THE SUPER-DUPER DUO

EASTER EGGSCAPADE

Story by Henri Meunier Illustrated by Nathalie Choux
Adapted by Liza Charlesworth

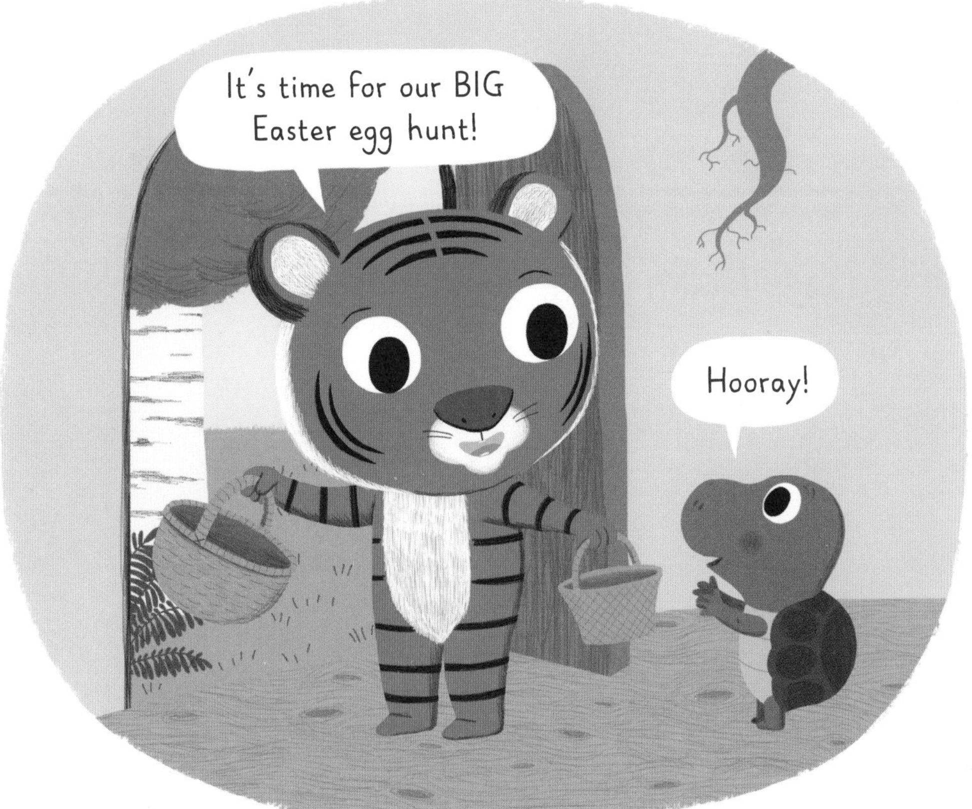
It's time for our BIG Easter egg hunt!
Hooray!

Houghton Mifflin Harcourt
Boston New York

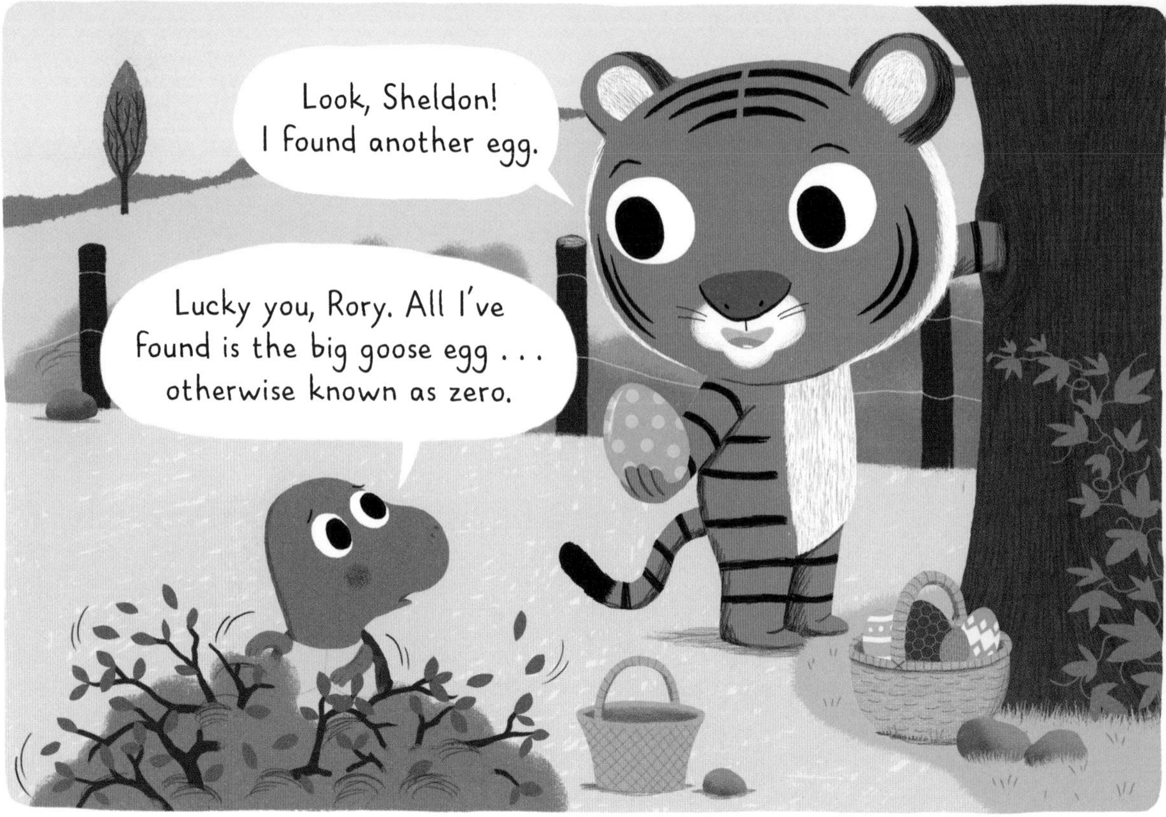
Look, Sheldon!
I found another egg.
Lucky you, Rory. All I've
found is the big goose egg . . .
otherwise known as zero.

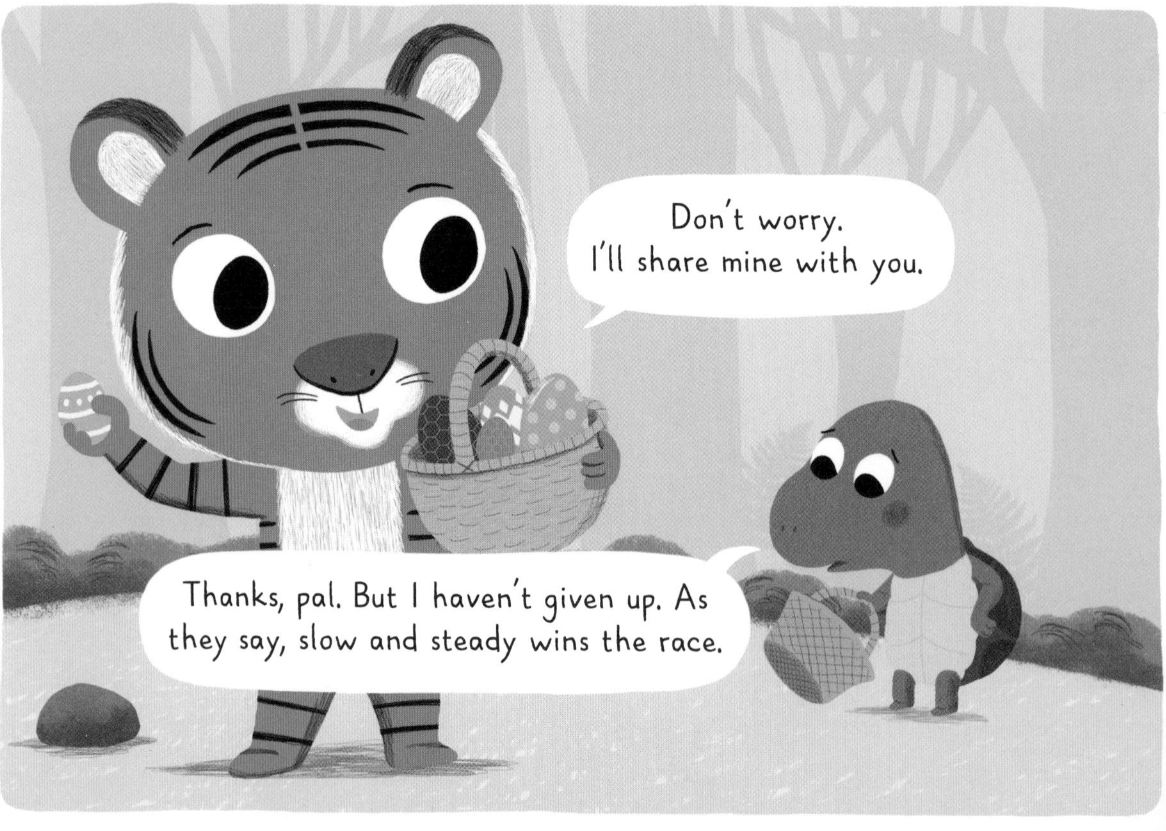
Don't worry.
I'll share mine with you.
Thanks, pal. But I haven't given up. As
they say, slow and steady wins the race.

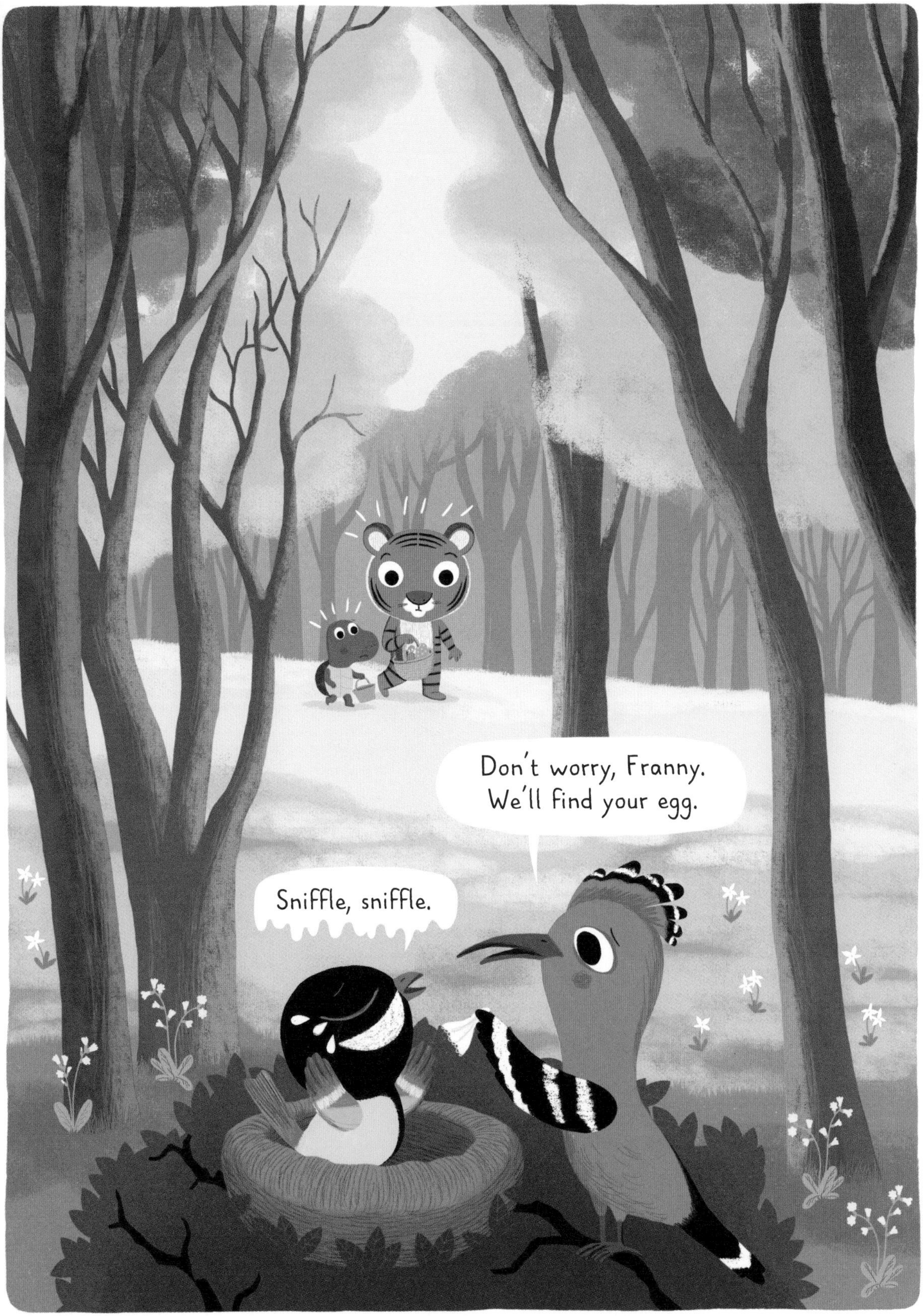
Sniffle, sniffle.
Don't worry, Franny. We'll find your egg.

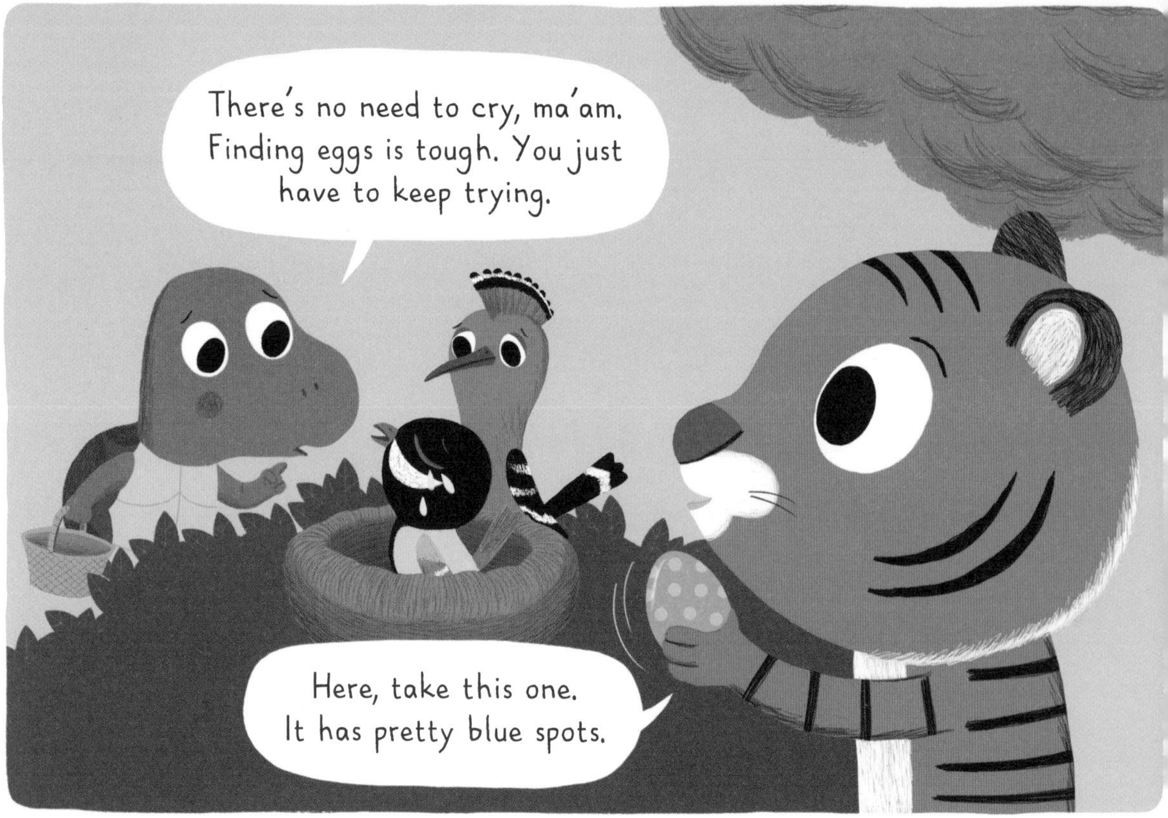
There's no need to cry, ma'am. Finding eggs is tough. You just have to keep trying.
Here, take this one. It has pretty blue spots.

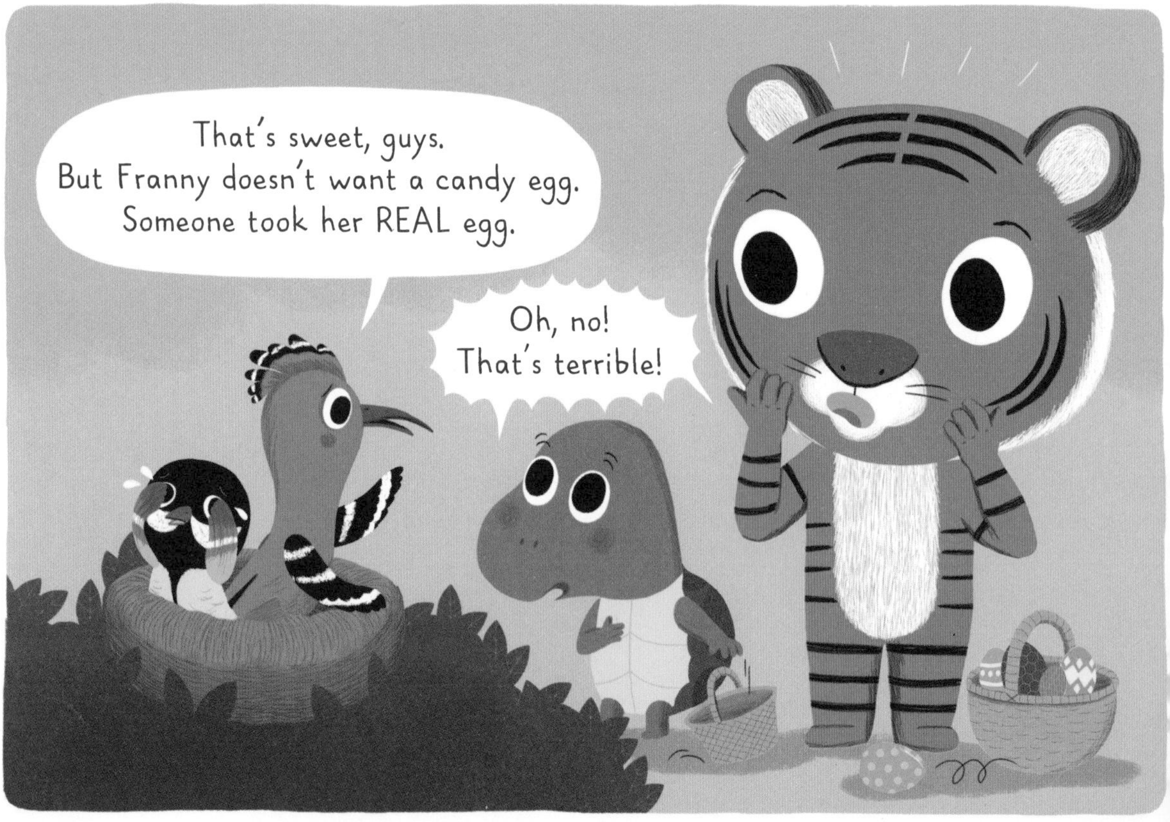
That's sweet, guys. But Franny doesn't want a candy egg. Someone took her REAL egg.
Oh, no! That's terrible!

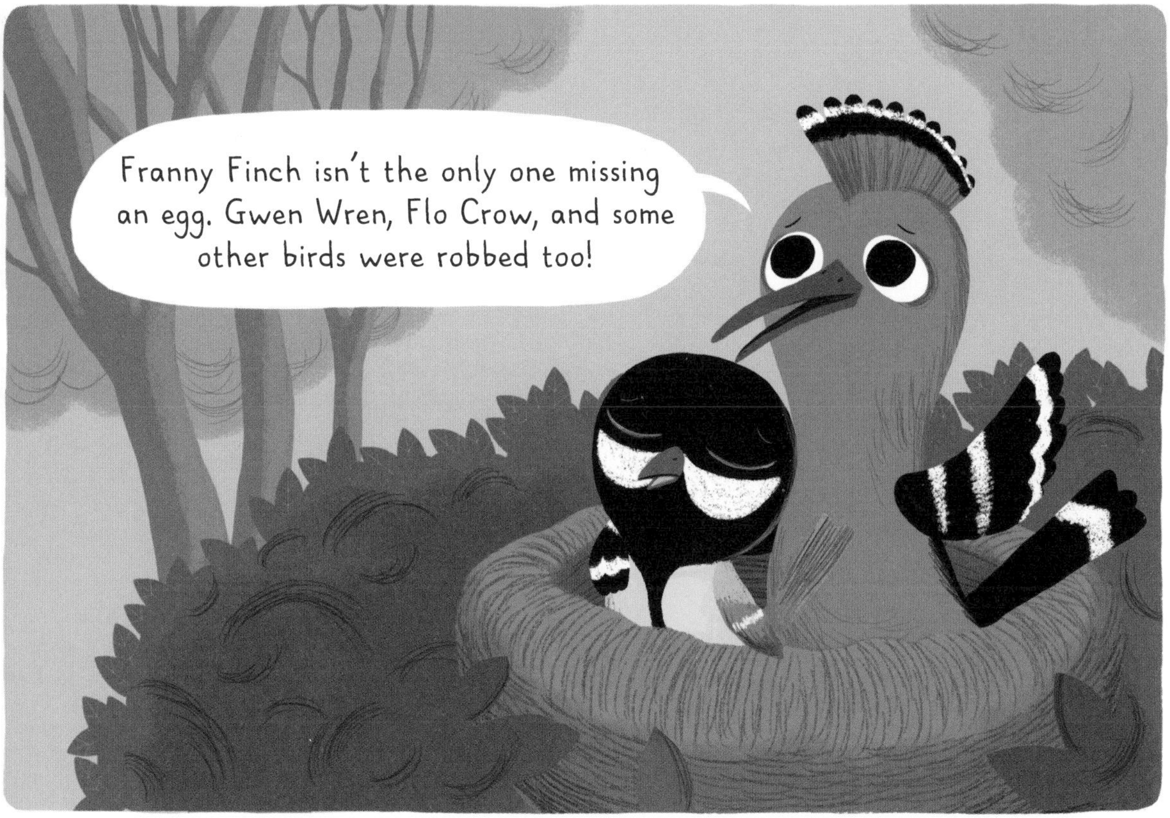
Franny Finch isn't the only one missing an egg. Gwen Wren, Flo Crow, and some other birds were robbed too!

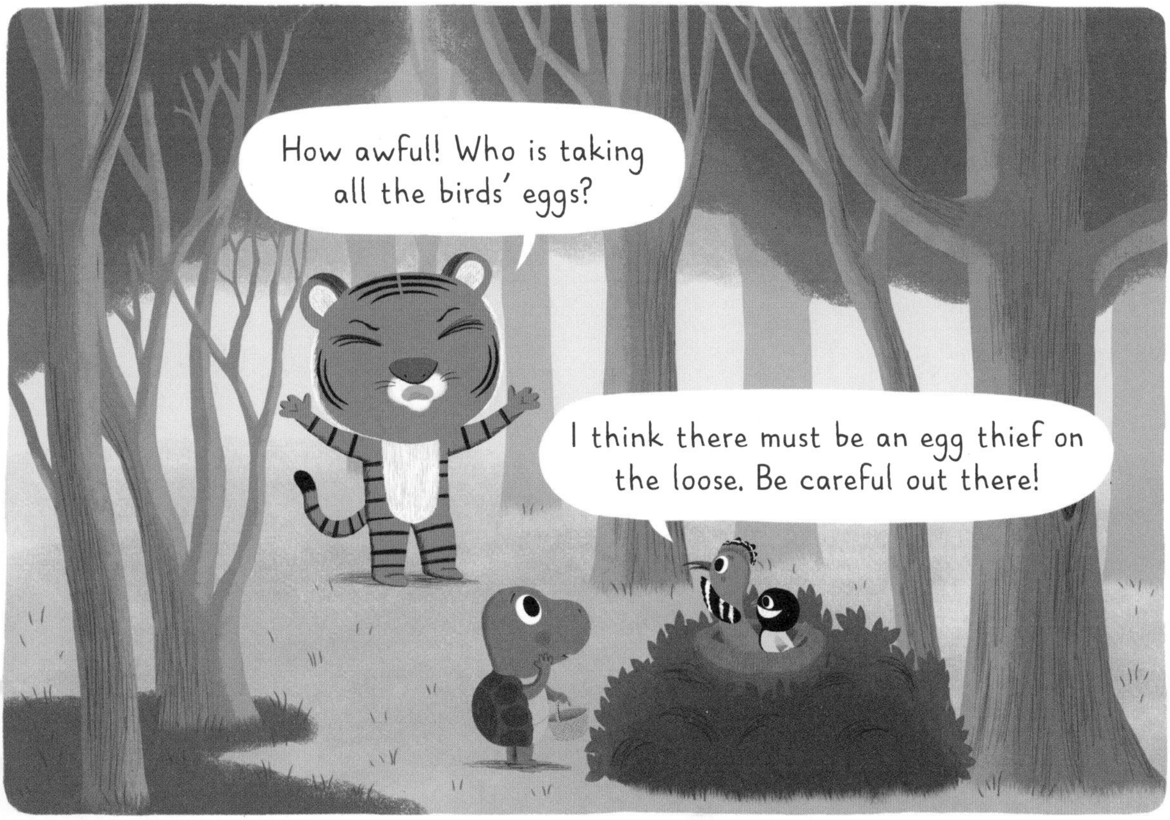
How awful! Who is taking all the birds' eggs?
I think there must be an egg thief on the loose. Be careful out there!

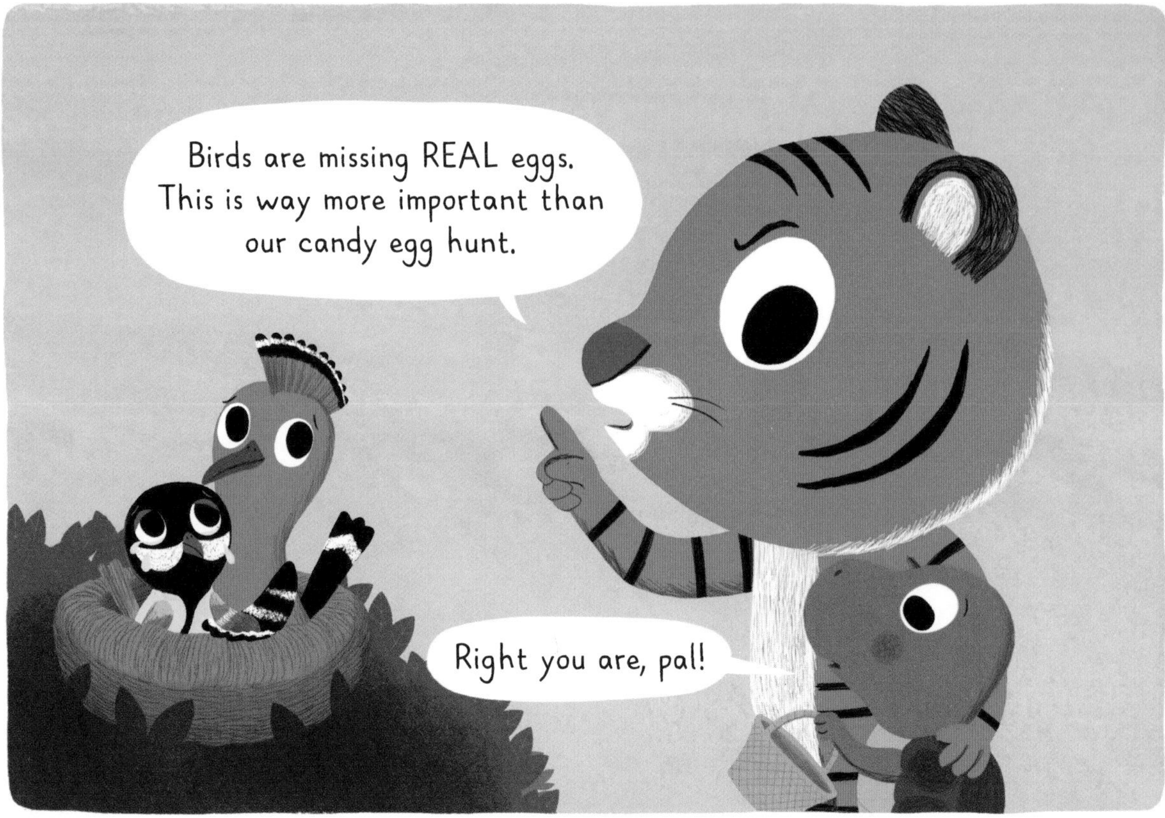
Birds are missing REAL eggs. This is way more important than our candy egg hunt.
Right you are, pal!

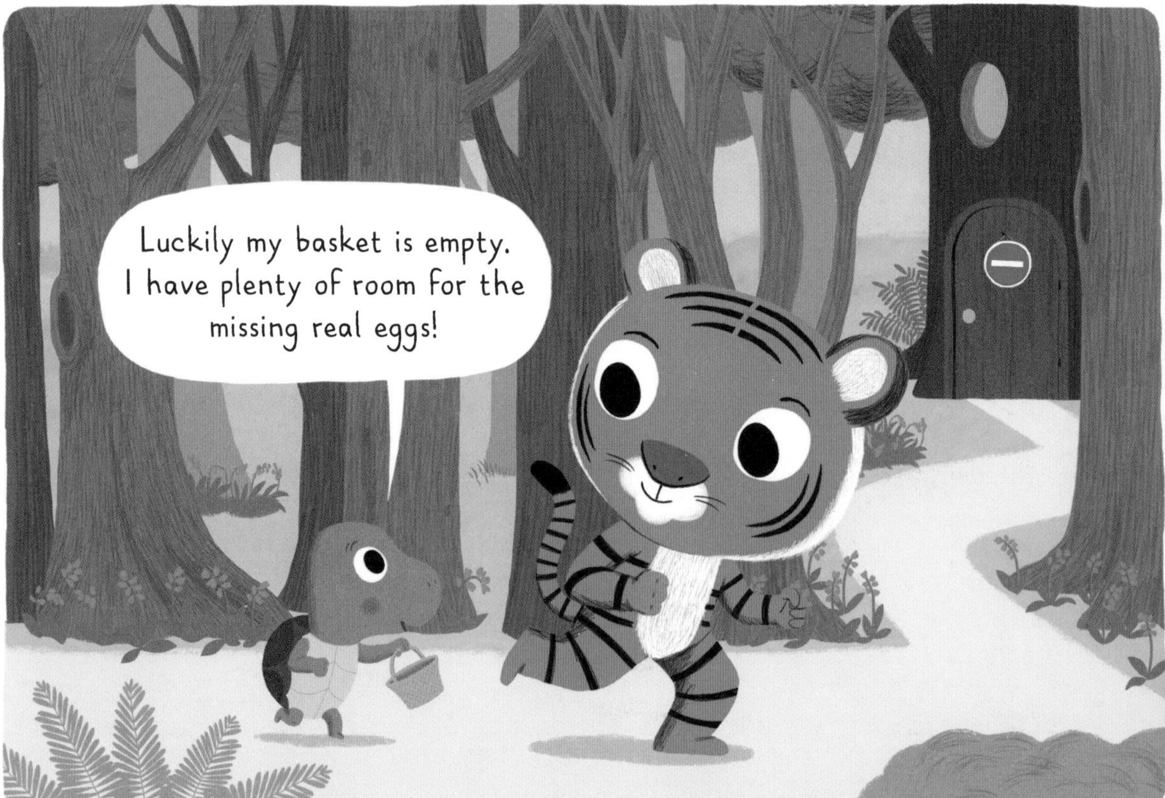
Luckily my basket is empty. I have plenty of room for the missing real eggs!

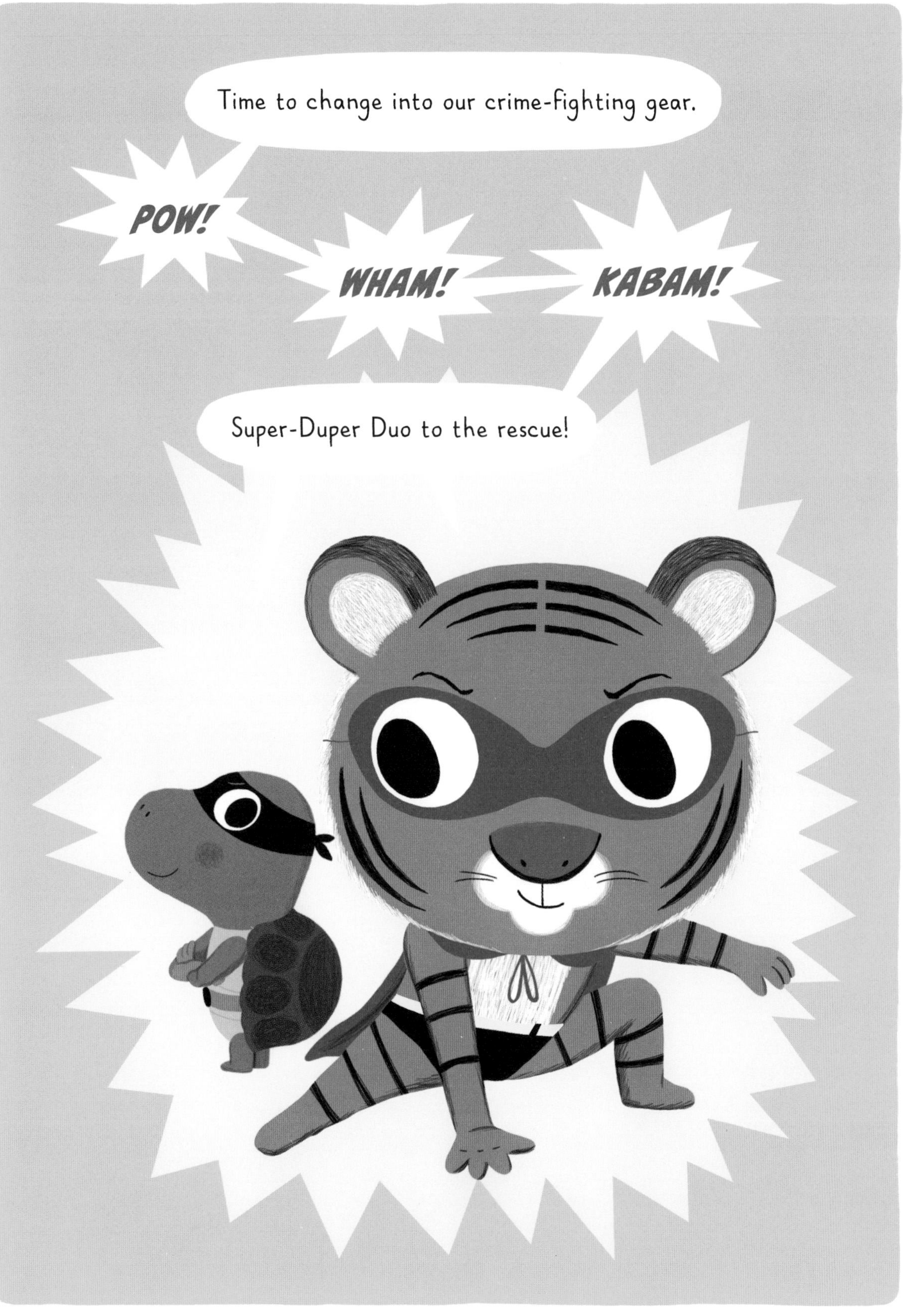
Time to change into our crime-fighting gear.
POW!
WHAM!
KABAM!
Super-Duper Duo to the rescue!

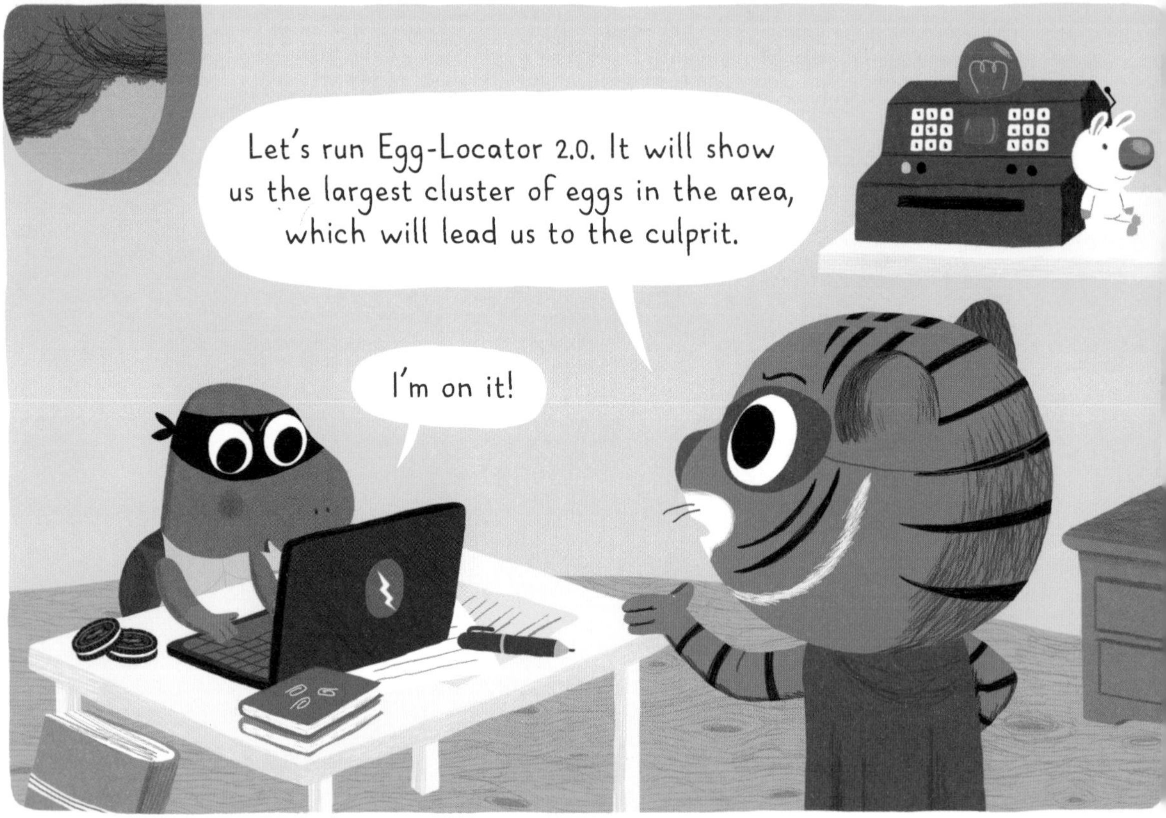
Let's run Egg-Locator 2.0. It will show us the largest cluster of eggs in the area, which will lead us to the culprit.
I'm on it!

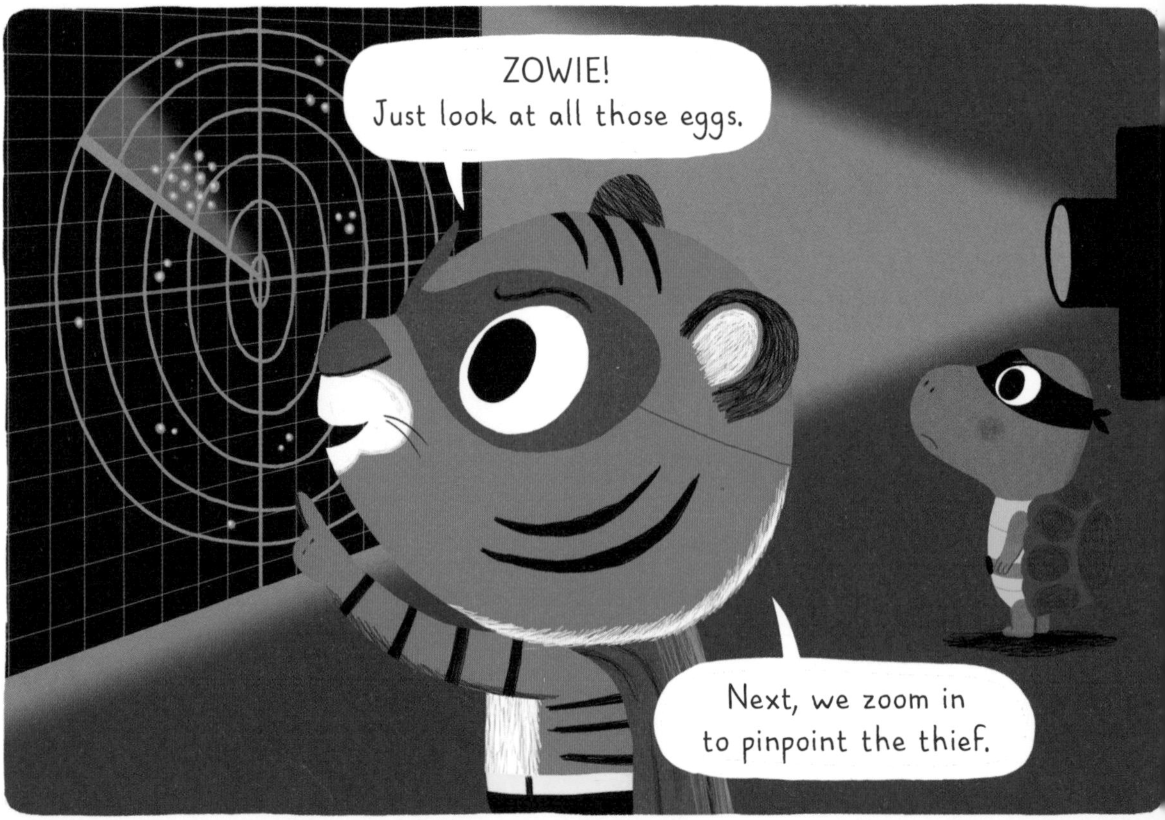
ZOWIE!
Just look at all those eggs.
Next, we zoom in to pinpoint the thief.

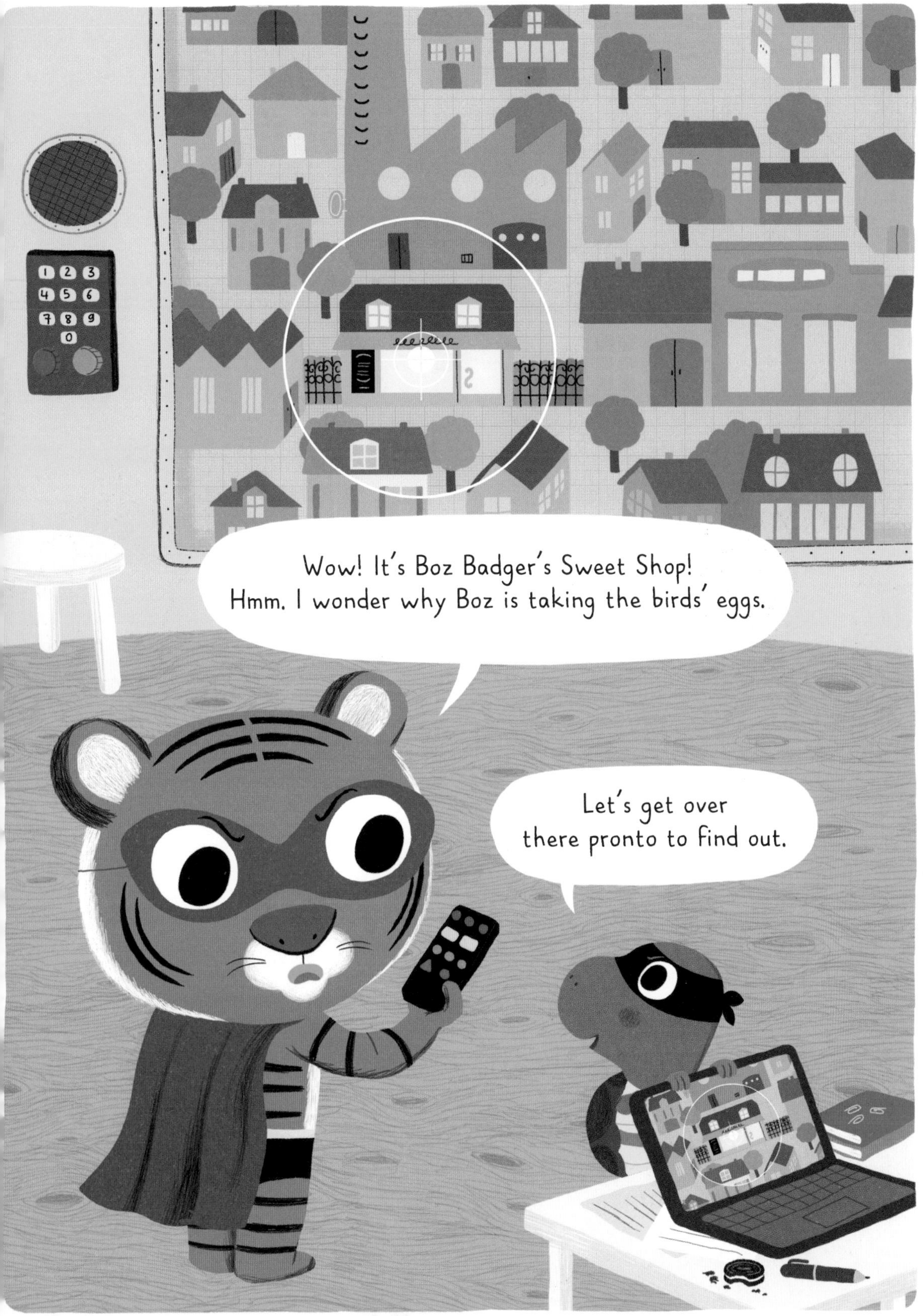
Wow! It's Boz Badger's Sweet Shop!
Hmm. I wonder why Boz is taking the birds' eggs.
Let's get over there pronto to find out.

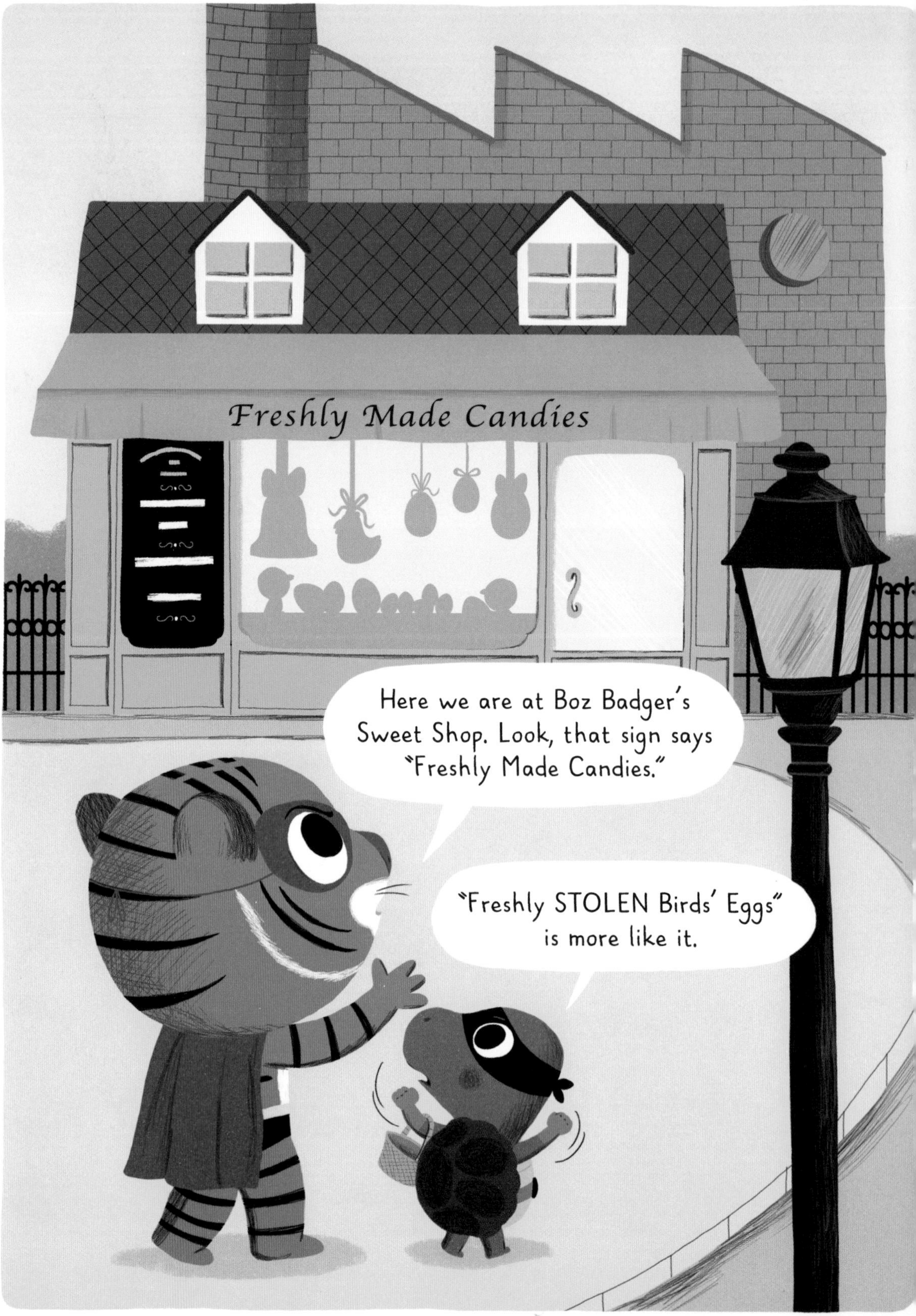
Freshly Made Candies
Here we are at Boz Badger's Sweet Shop. Look, that sign says "Freshly Made Candies."
"Freshly STOLEN Birds' Eggs" is more like it.

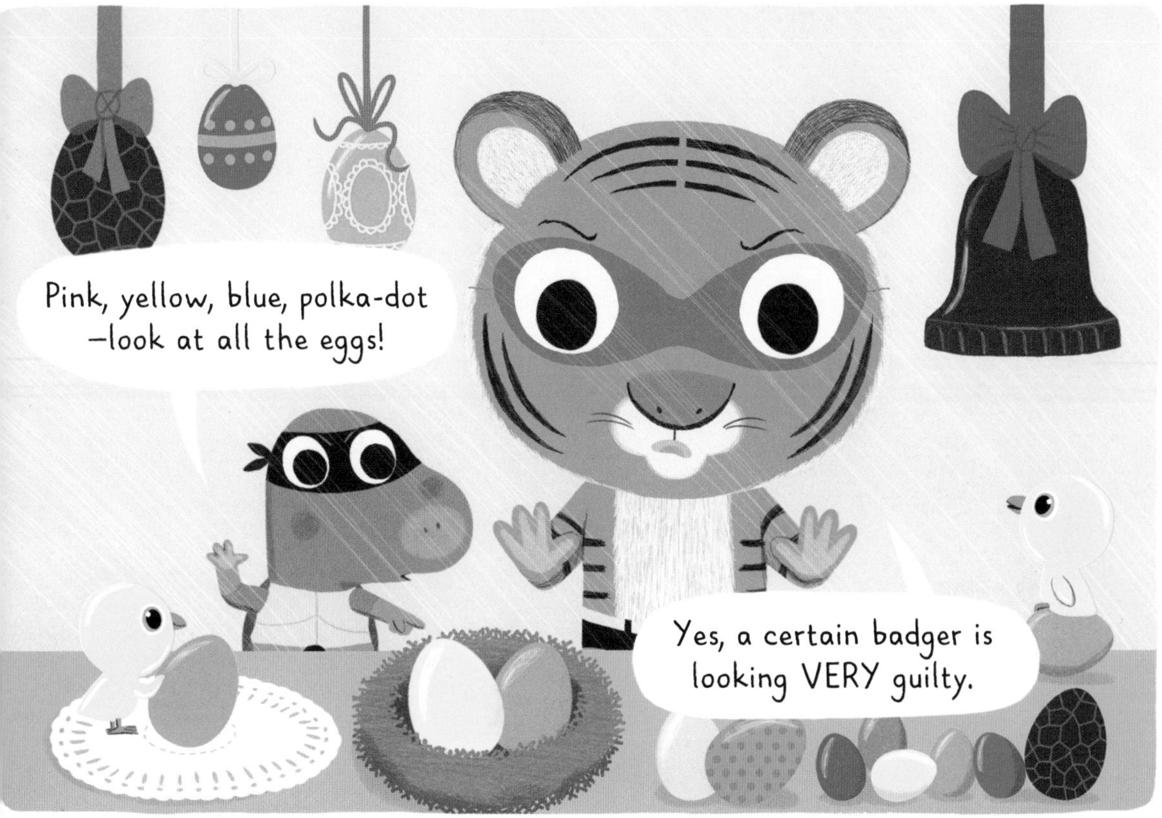
Pink, yellow, blue, polka-dot —look at all the eggs!
Yes, a certain badger is looking VERY guilty.

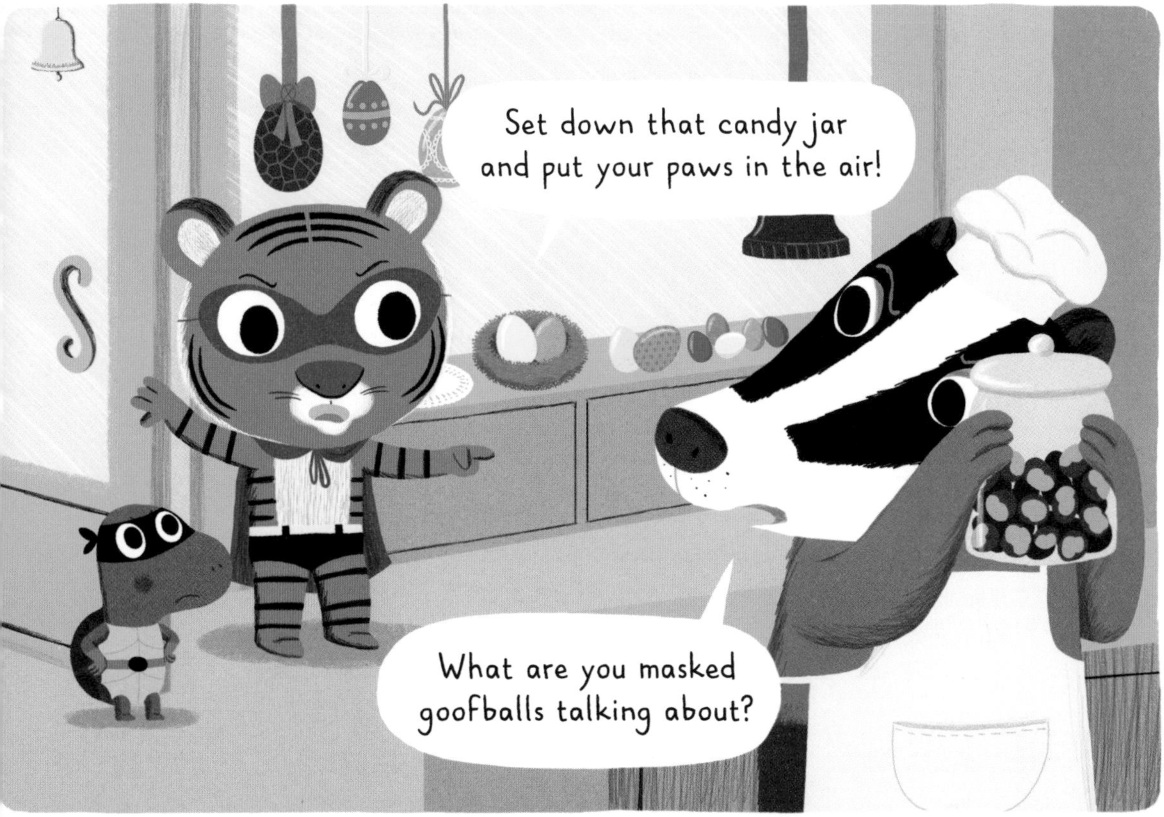
Set down that candy jar and put your paws in the air!
What are you masked goofballs talking about?

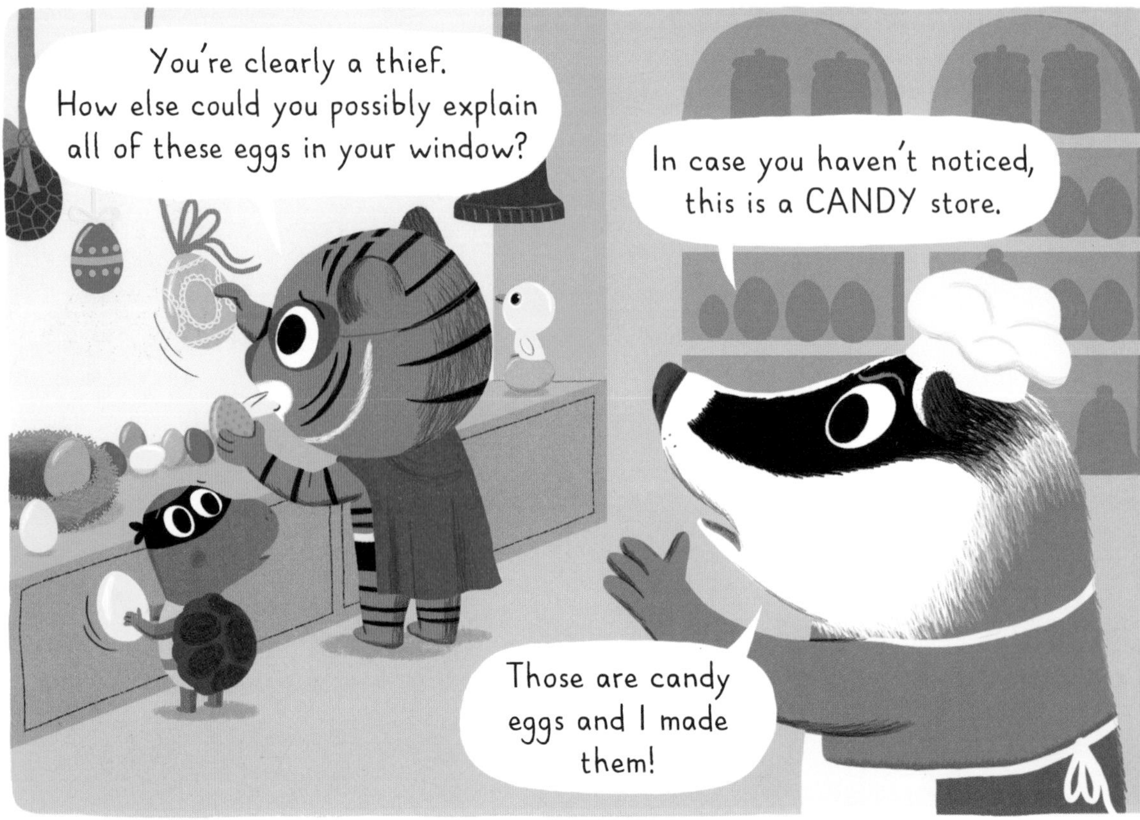
You're clearly a thief. How else could you possibly explain all of these eggs in your window?
In case you haven't noticed, this is a CANDY store.
Those are candy eggs and I made them!

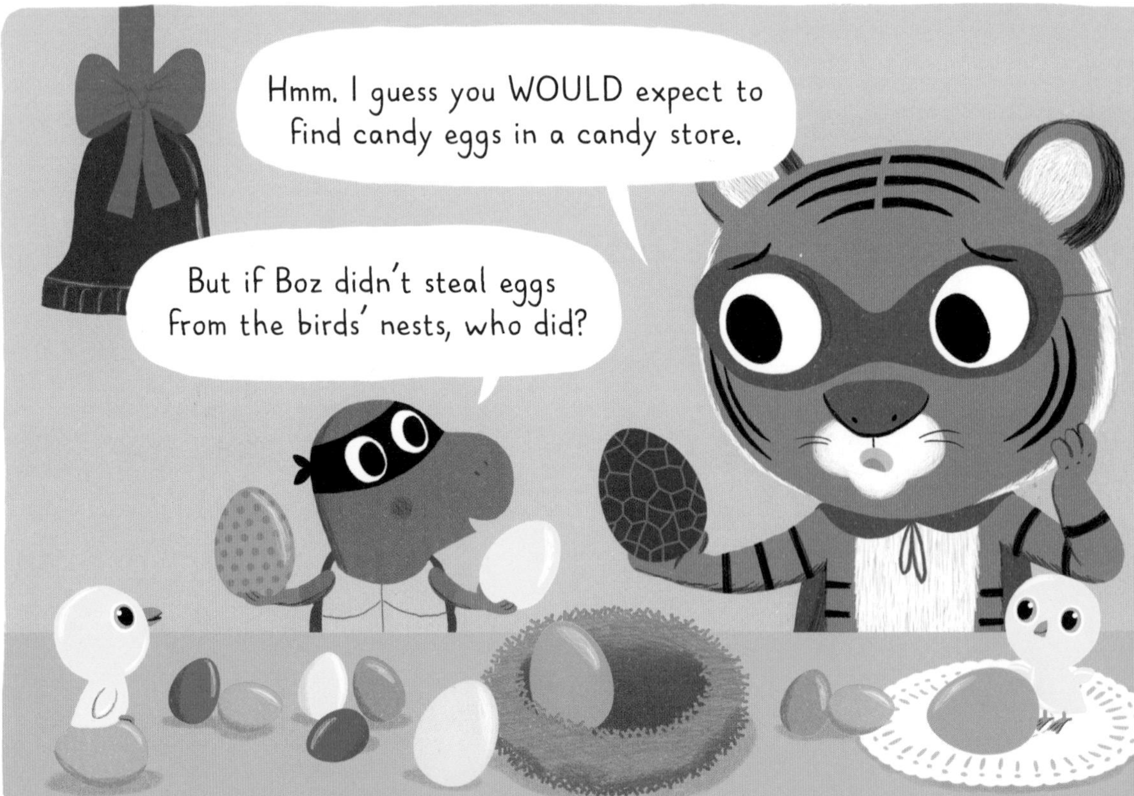
Hmm. I guess you WOULD expect to find candy eggs in a candy store.
But if Boz didn't steal eggs from the birds' nests, who did?

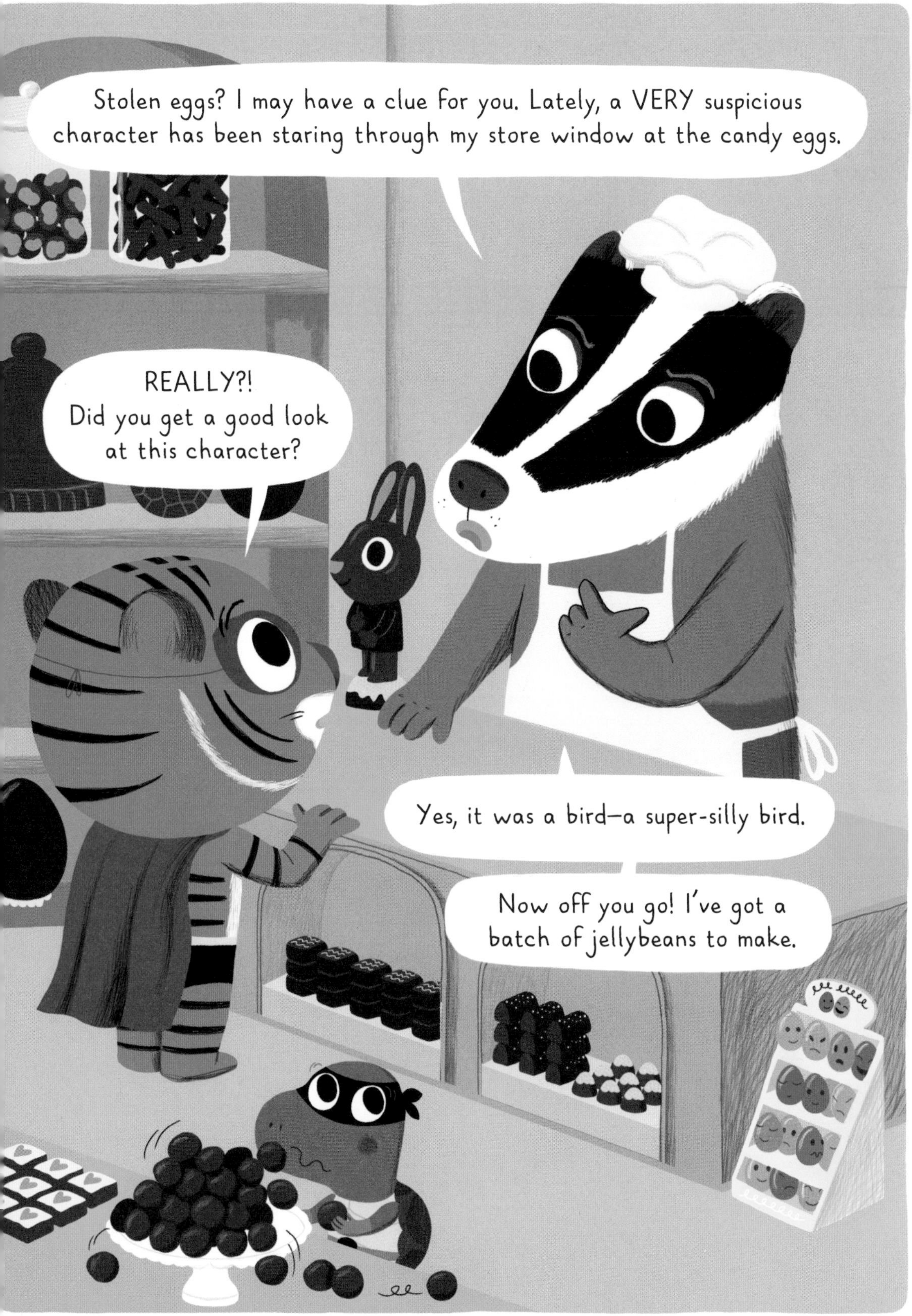
Stolen eggs? I may have a clue for you. Lately, a VERY suspicious character has been staring through my store window at the candy eggs.
REALLY?! Did you get a good look at this character?
Yes, it was a bird—a super-silly bird.
Now off you go! I've got a batch of jellybeans to make.

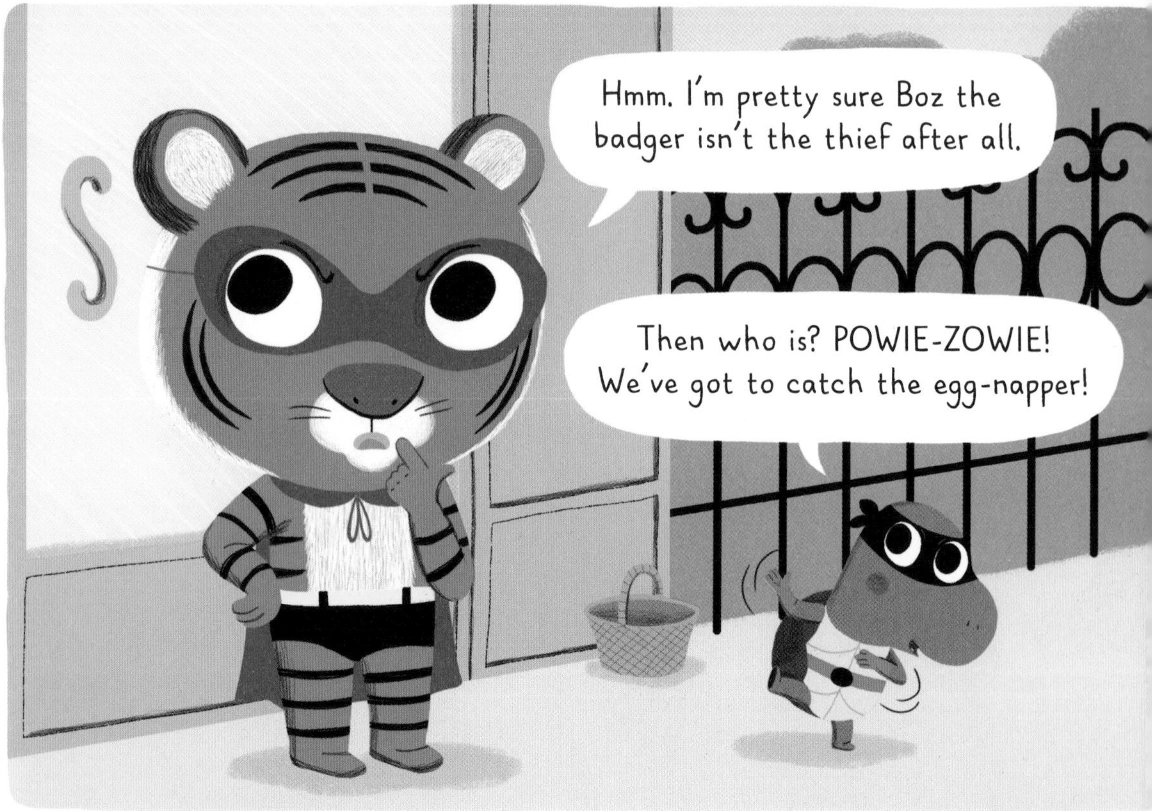
Hmm. I'm pretty sure Boz the badger isn't the thief after all.
Then who is? POWIE-ZOWIE! We've got to catch the egg-napper!

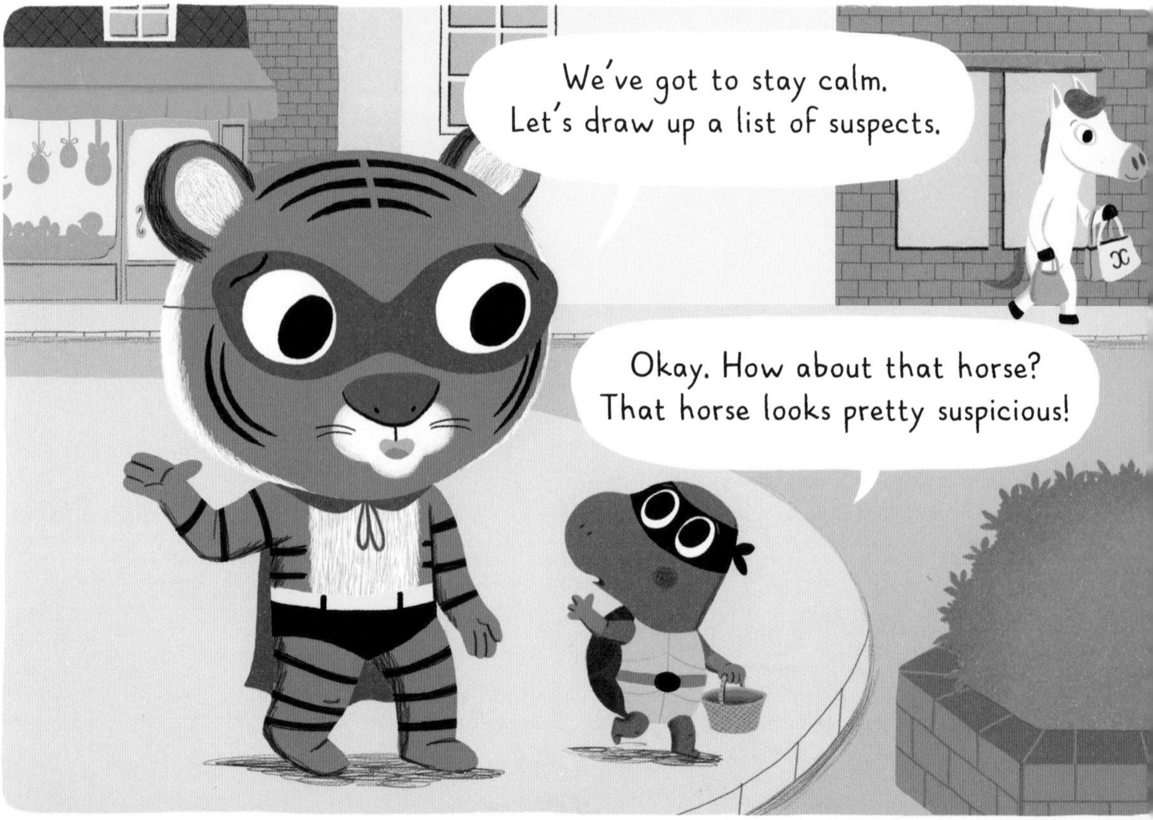
We've got to stay calm. Let's draw up a list of suspects.
Okay. How about that horse? That horse looks pretty suspicious!

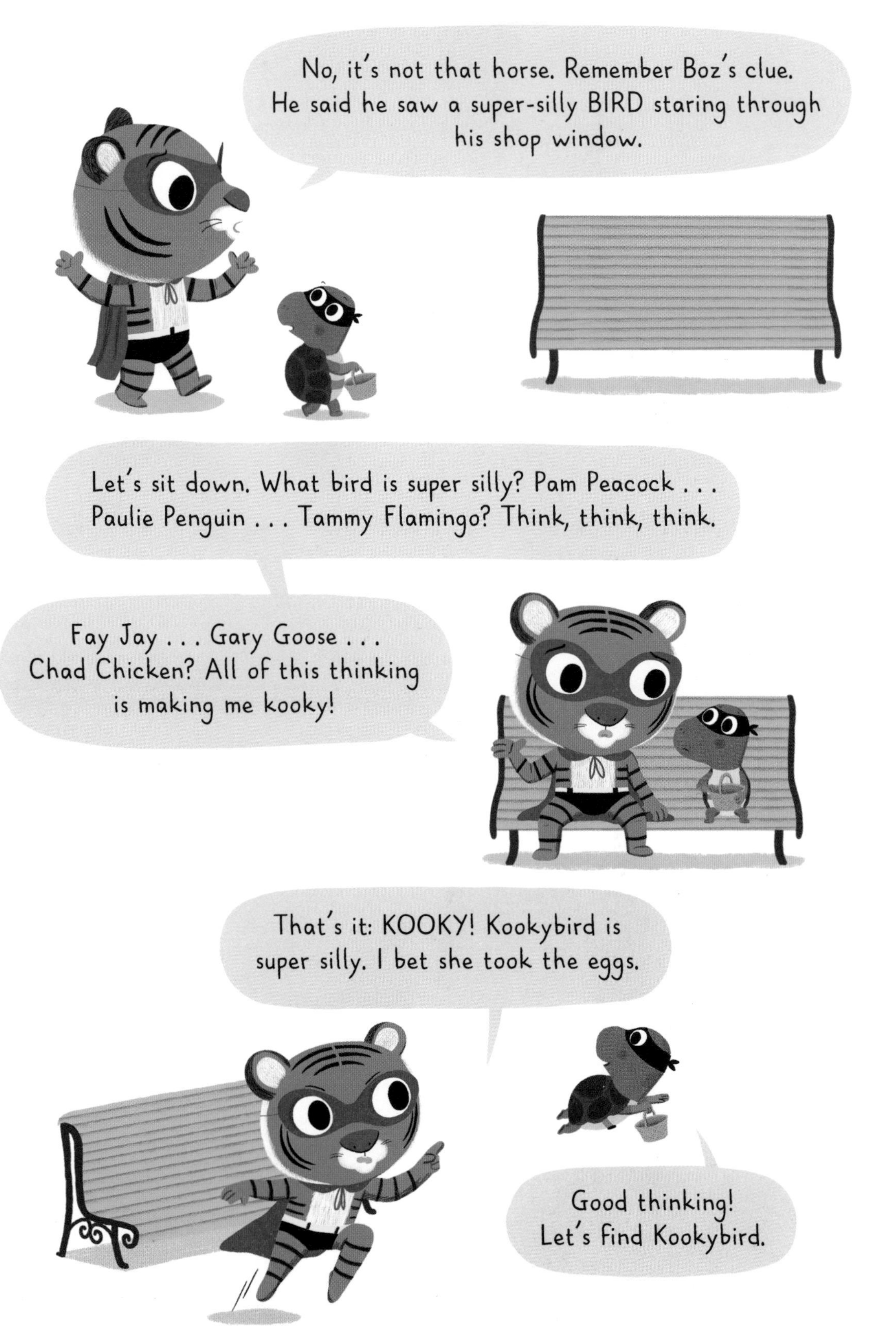
No, it's not that horse. Remember Boz's clue. He said he saw a super-silly BIRD staring through his shop window.
Let's sit down. What bird is super silly? Pam Peacock . . . Paulie Penguin . . . Tammy Flamingo? Think, think, think.
Fay Jay . . . Gary Goose . . . Chad Chicken? All of this thinking is making me kooky!
That's it: KOOKY! Kookybird is super silly. I bet she took the eggs.
Good thinking! Let's find Kookybird.

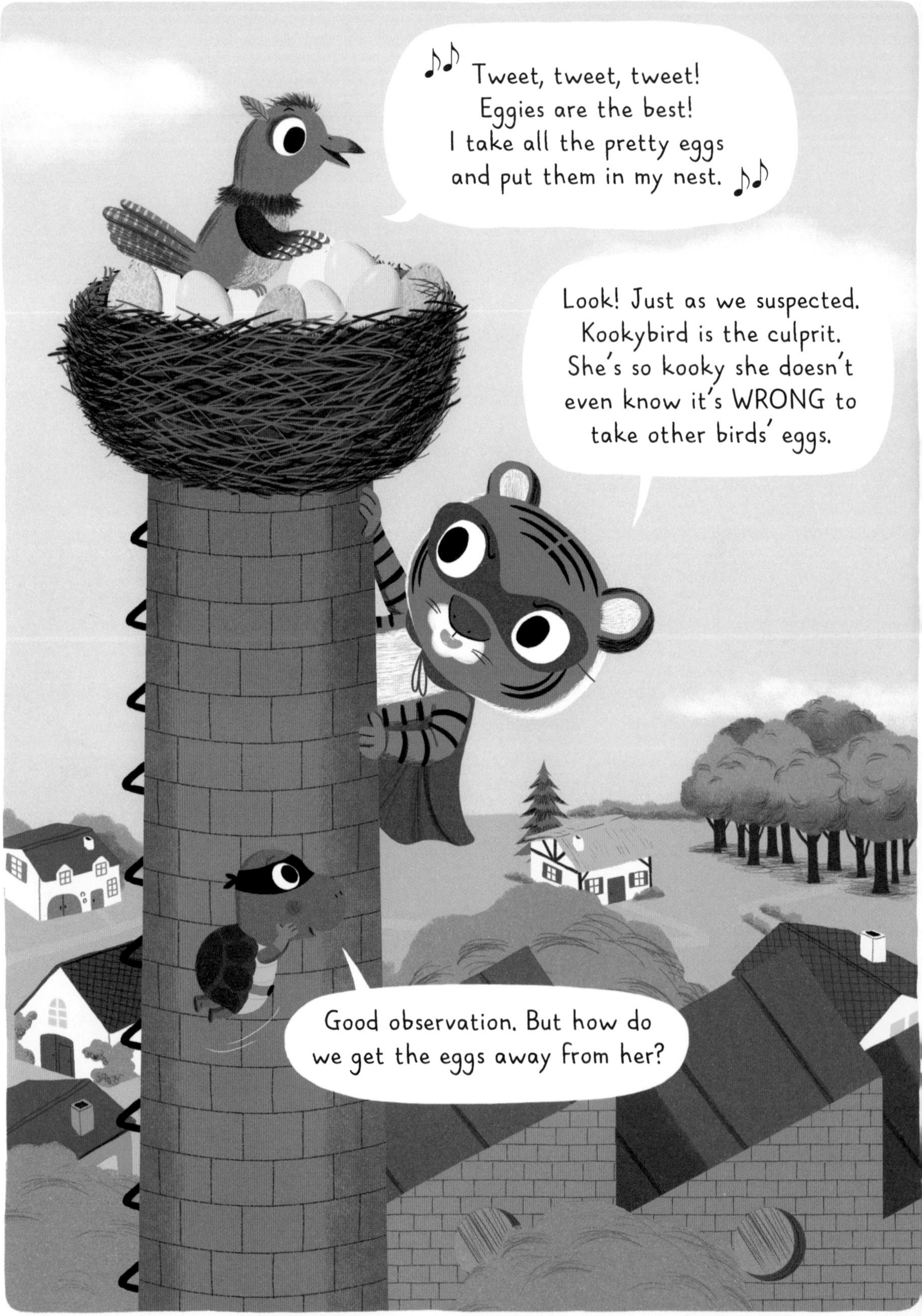
Tweet, tweet, tweet! Eggies are the best! I take all the pretty eggs and put them in my nest.
Look! Just as we suspected. Kookybird is the culprit. She's so kooky she doesn't even know it's WRONG to take other birds' eggs.
Good observation. But how do we get the eggs away from her?

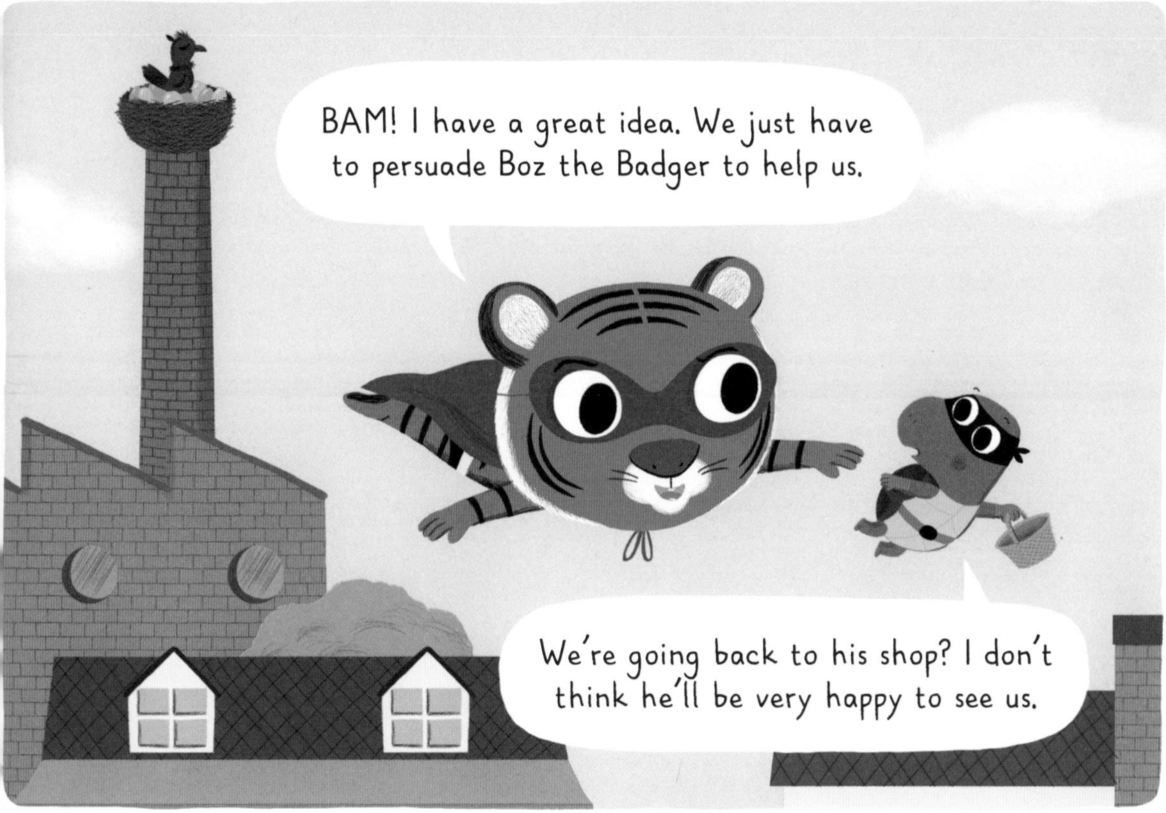
BAM! I have a great idea. We just have to persuade Boz the Badger to help us.
We're going back to his shop? I don't think he'll be very happy to see us.

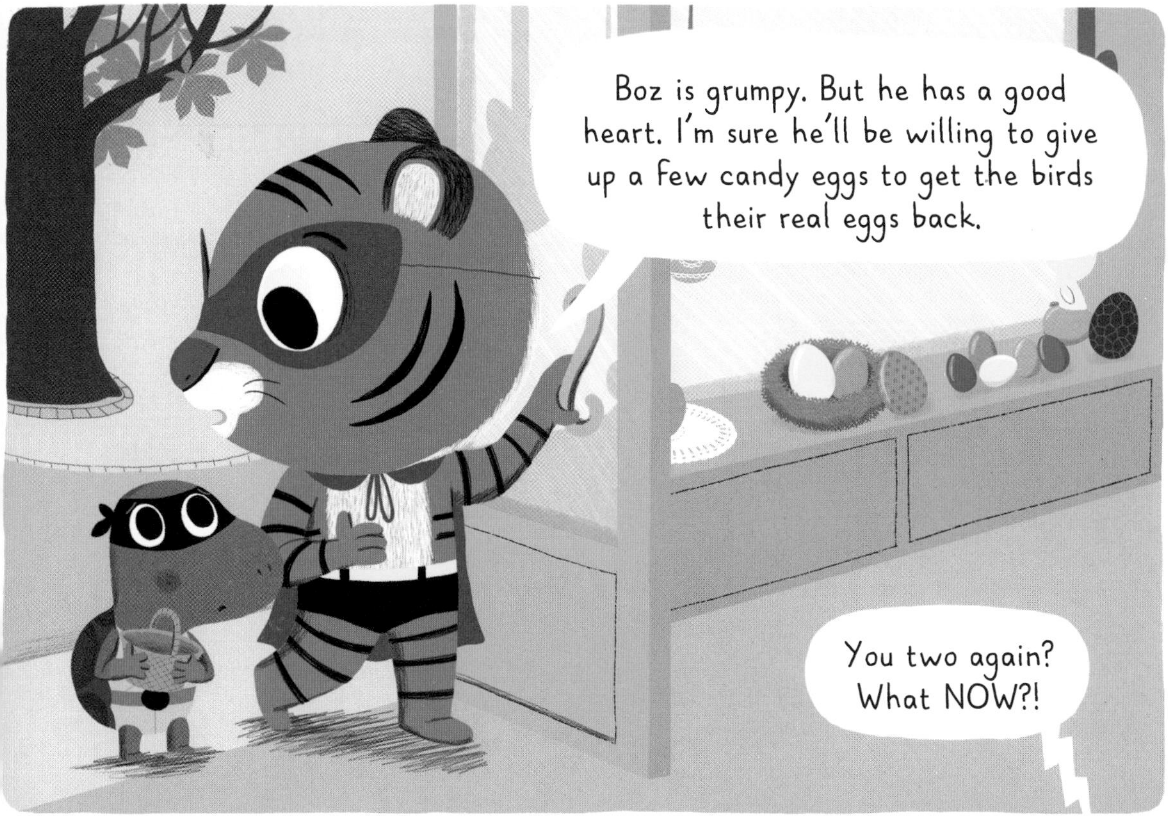
Boz is grumpy. But he has a good heart. I'm sure he'll be willing to give up a few candy eggs to get the birds their real eggs back.
You two again? What NOW?!

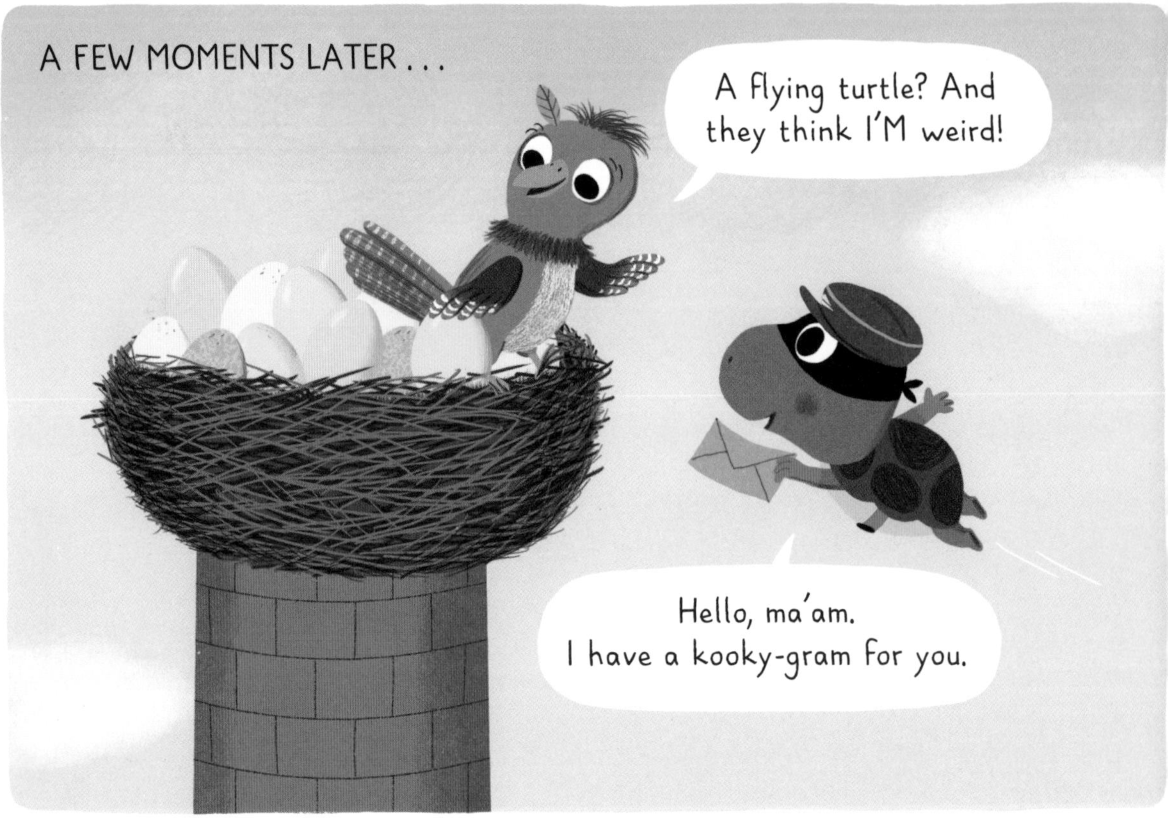
A FEW MOMENTS LATER . . .
A flying turtle? And they think I'M weird!
Hello, ma'am. I have a kooky-gram for you.

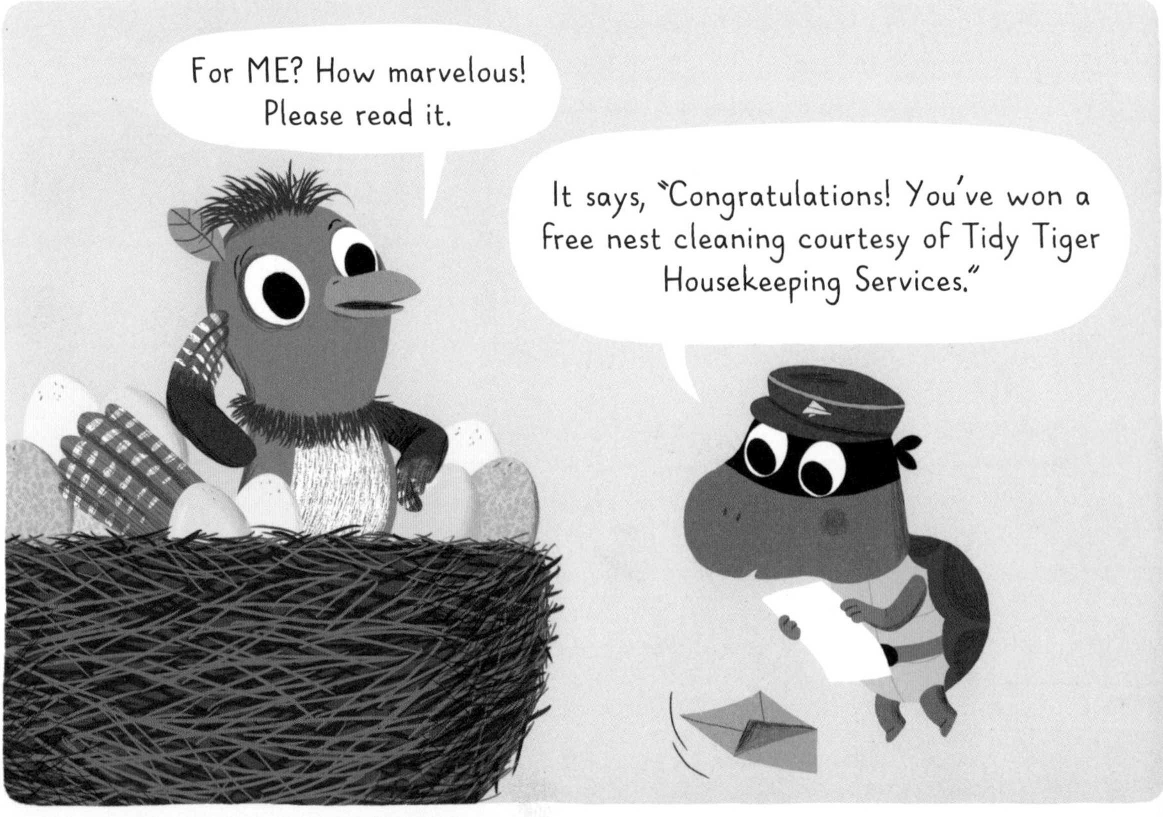
For ME? How marvelous! Please read it.
It says, "Congratulations! You've won a free nest cleaning courtesy of Tidy Tiger Housekeeping Services."

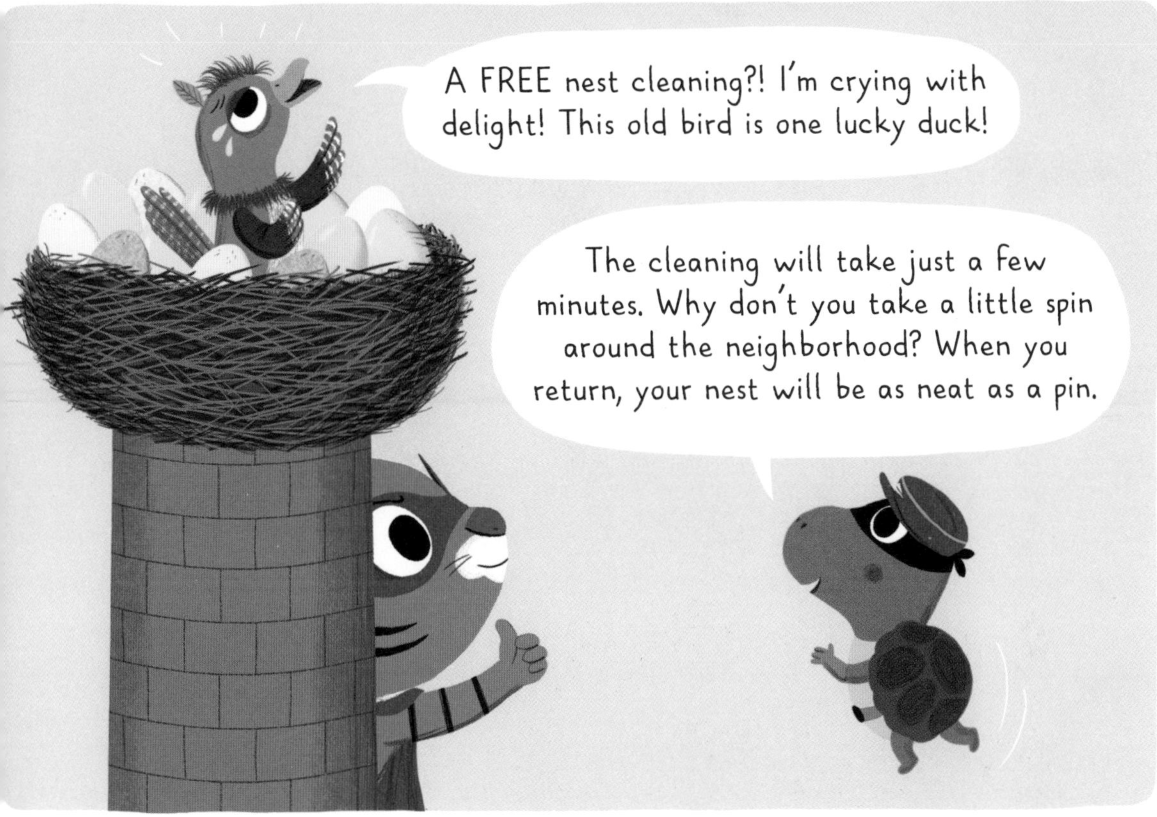
A FREE nest cleaning?! I'm crying with delight! This old bird is one lucky duck!
The cleaning will take just a few minutes. Why don't you take a little spin around the neighborhood? When you return, your nest will be as neat as a pin.

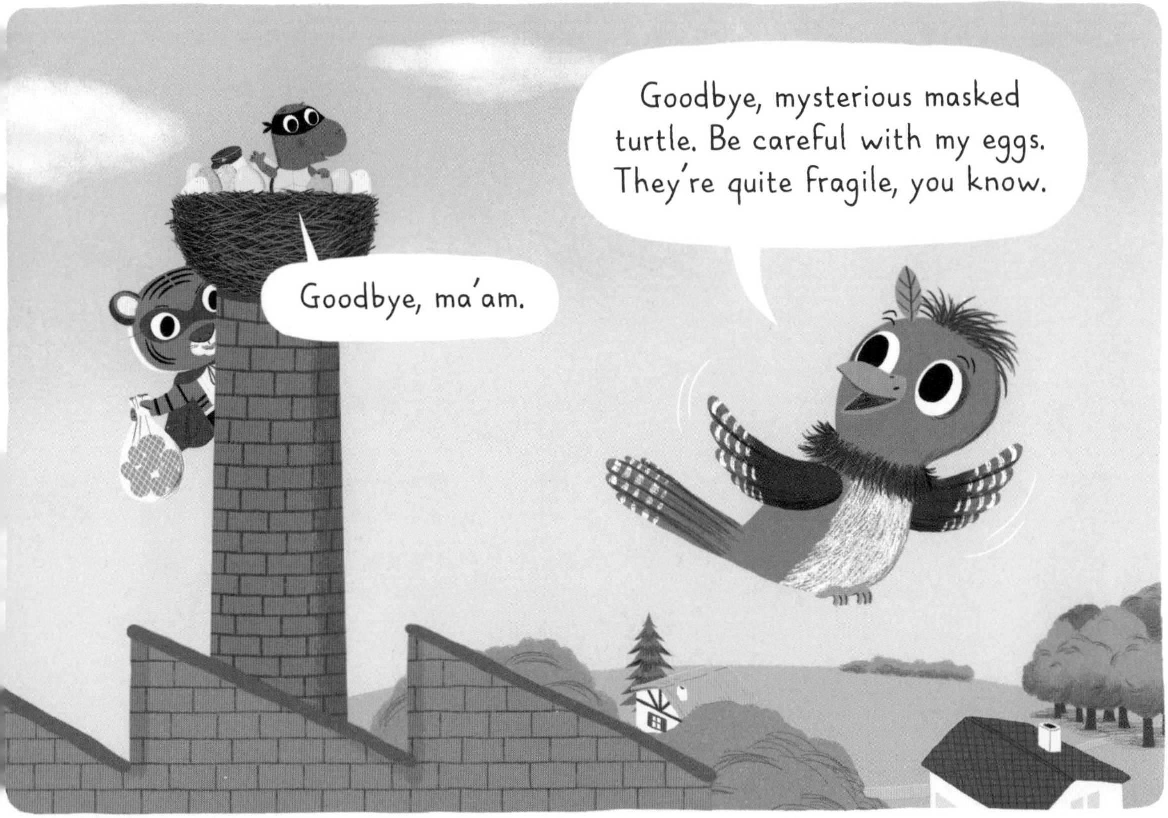
Goodbye, mysterious masked turtle. Be careful with my eggs. They're quite fragile, you know.
Goodbye, ma'am.

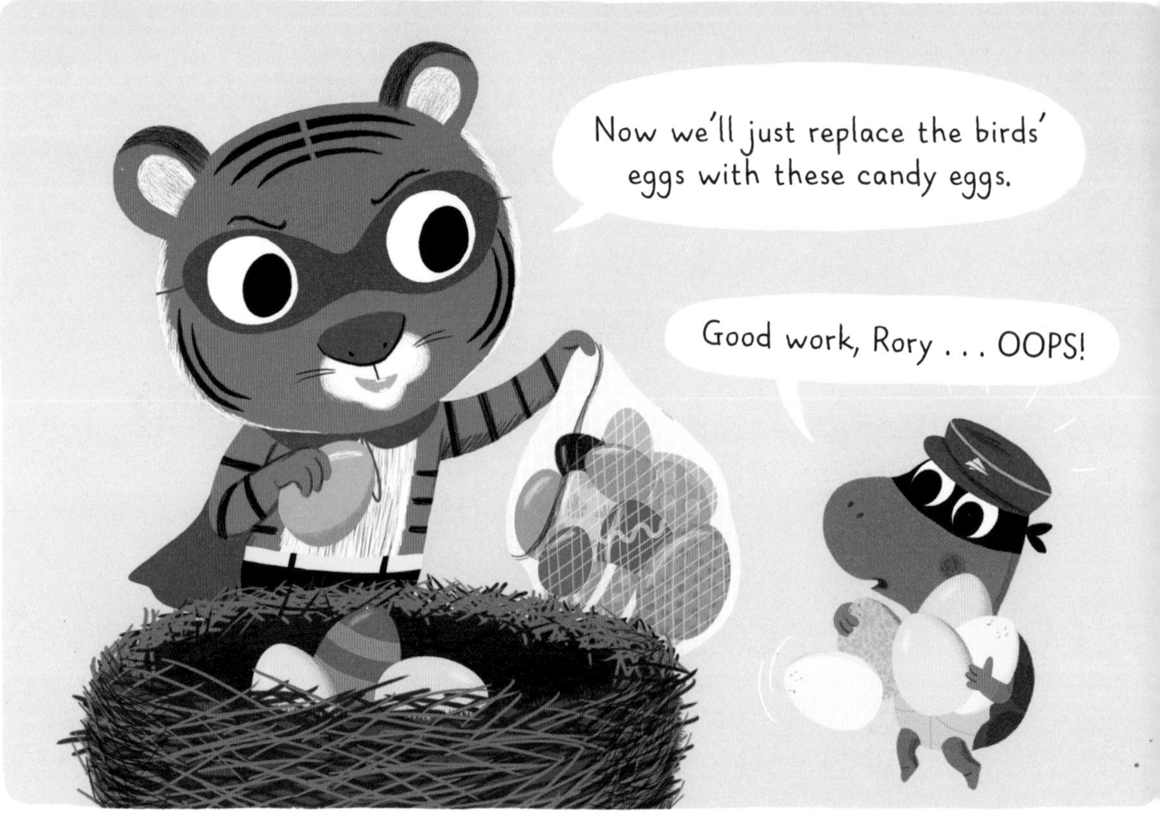
Now we'll just replace the birds' eggs with these candy eggs.
Good work, Rory . . . OOPS!

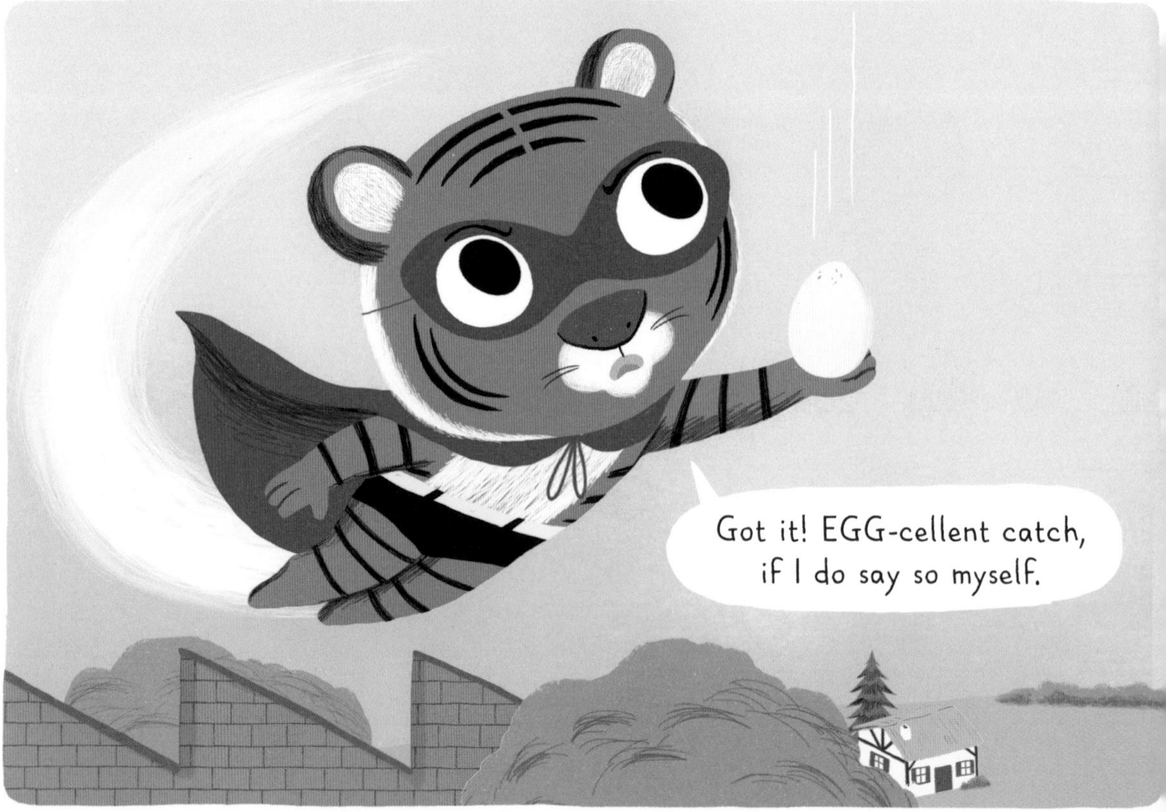
Got it! EGG-cellent catch, if I do say so myself.

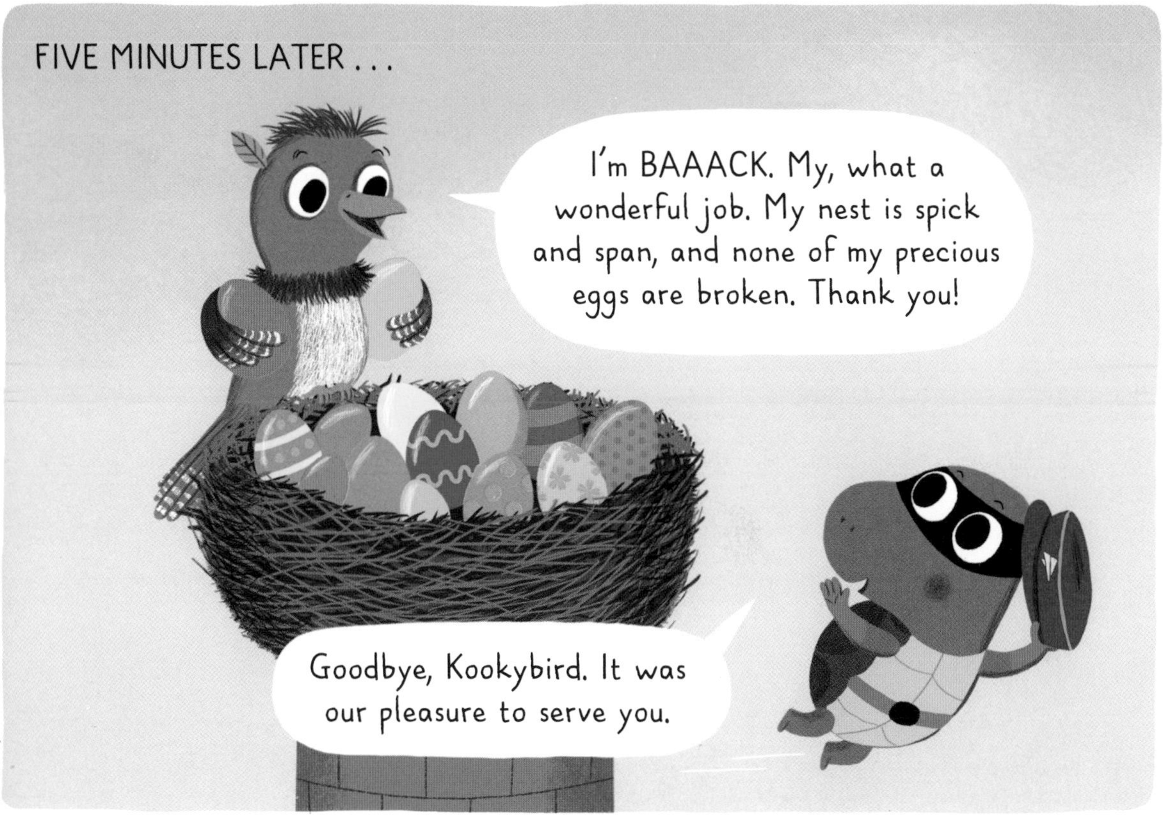
FIVE MINUTES LATER . . .
I'm BAAACK. My, what a wonderful job. My nest is spick and span, and none of my precious eggs are broken. Thank you!
Goodbye, Kookybird. It was our pleasure to serve you.

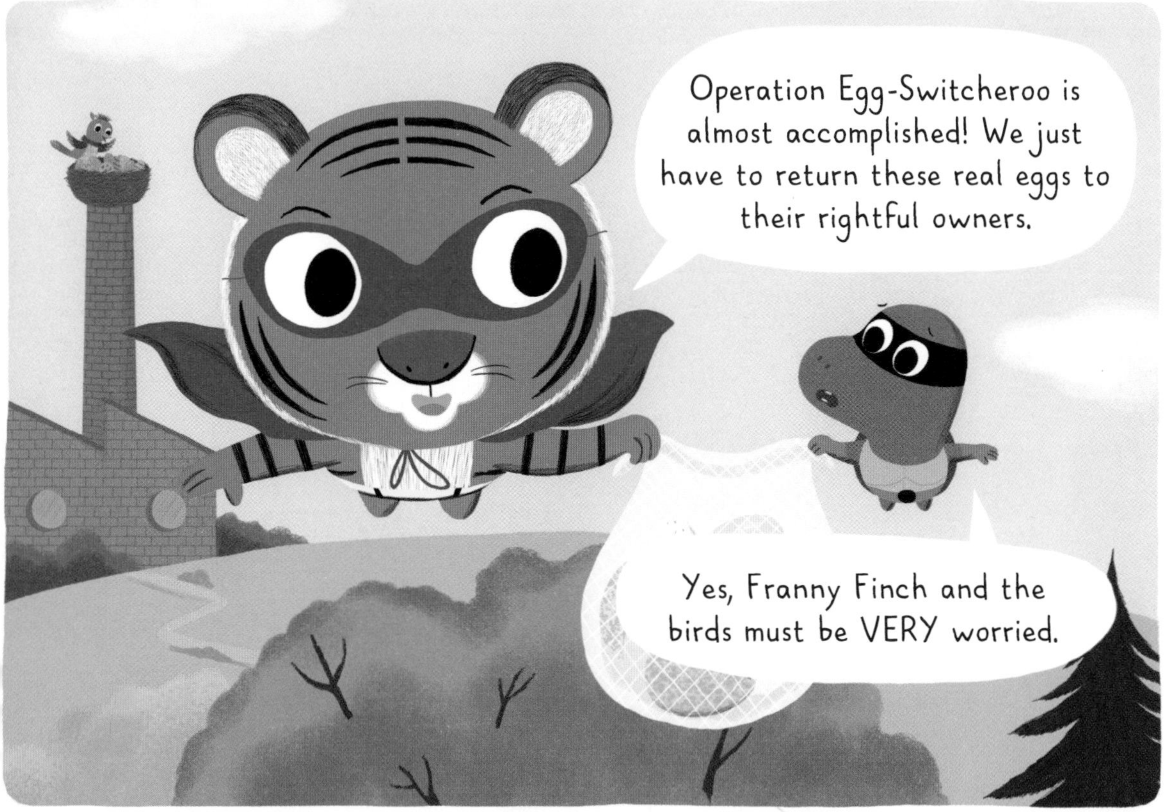
Operation Egg-Switcheroo is almost accomplished! We just have to return these real eggs to their rightful owners.
Yes, Franny Finch and the birds must be VERY worried.

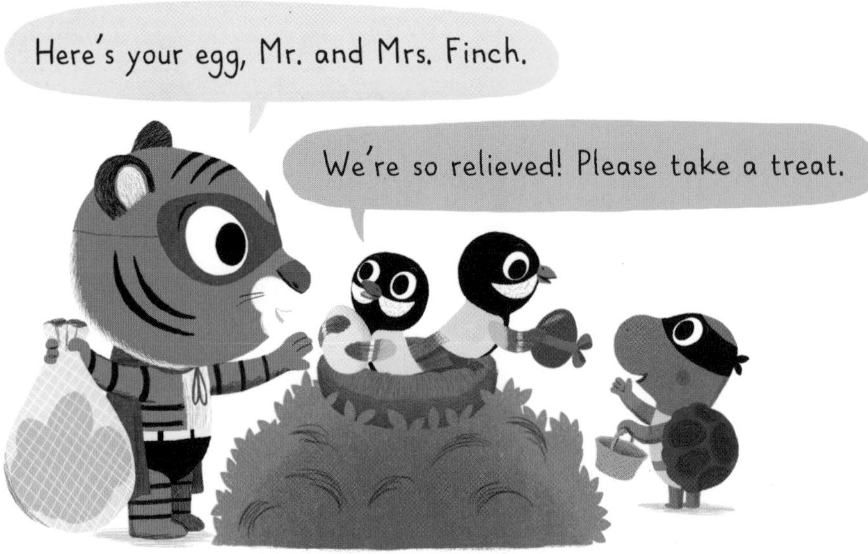
Here's your egg, Mr. and Mrs. Finch.
We're so relieved! Please take a treat.

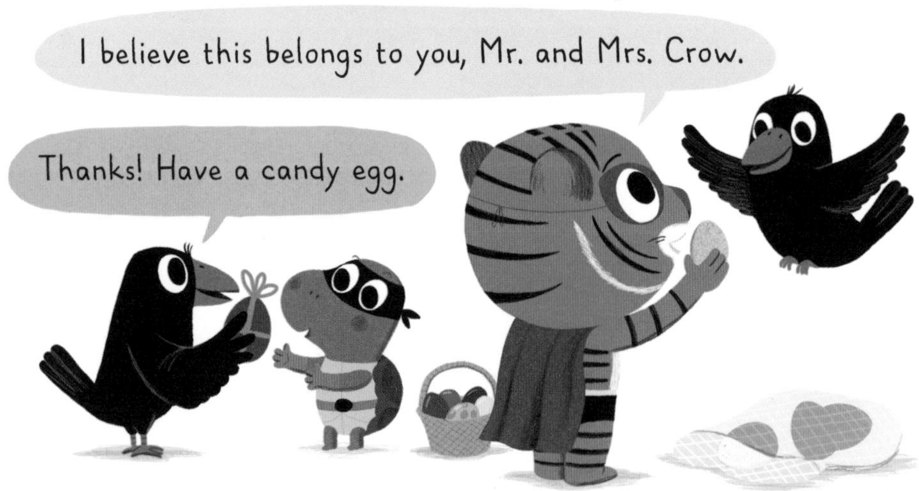
I believe this belongs to you, Mr. and Mrs. Crow.
Thanks! Have a candy egg.

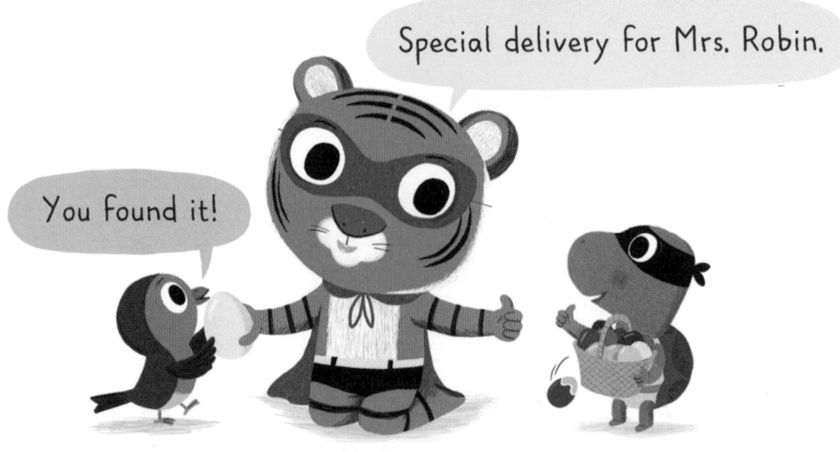
Special delivery for Mrs. Robin.
You found it!

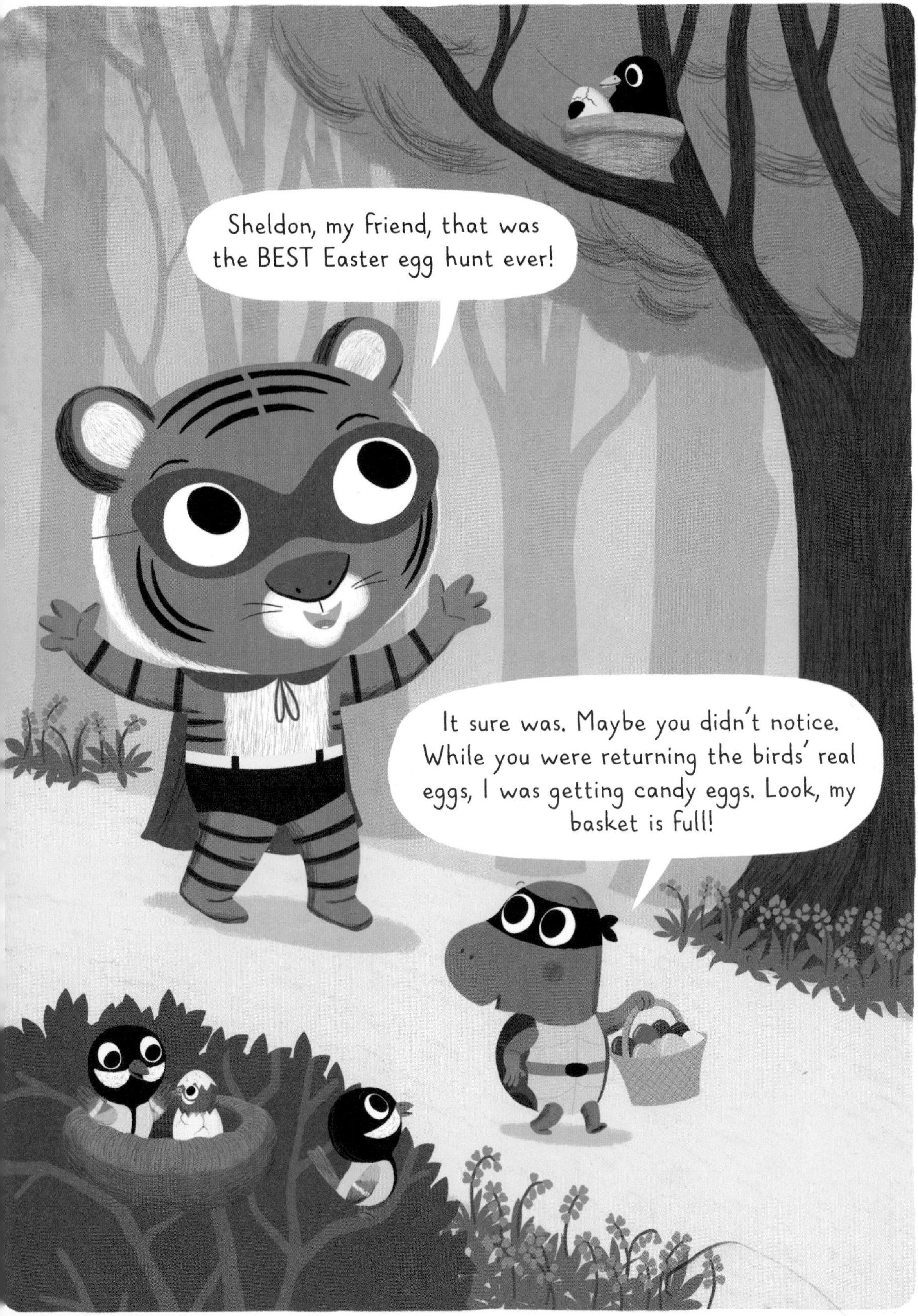

Sheldon, my friend, that was the BEST Easter egg hunt ever!
It sure was. Maybe you didn't notice. While you were returning the birds' real eggs, I was getting candy eggs. Look, my basket is full!

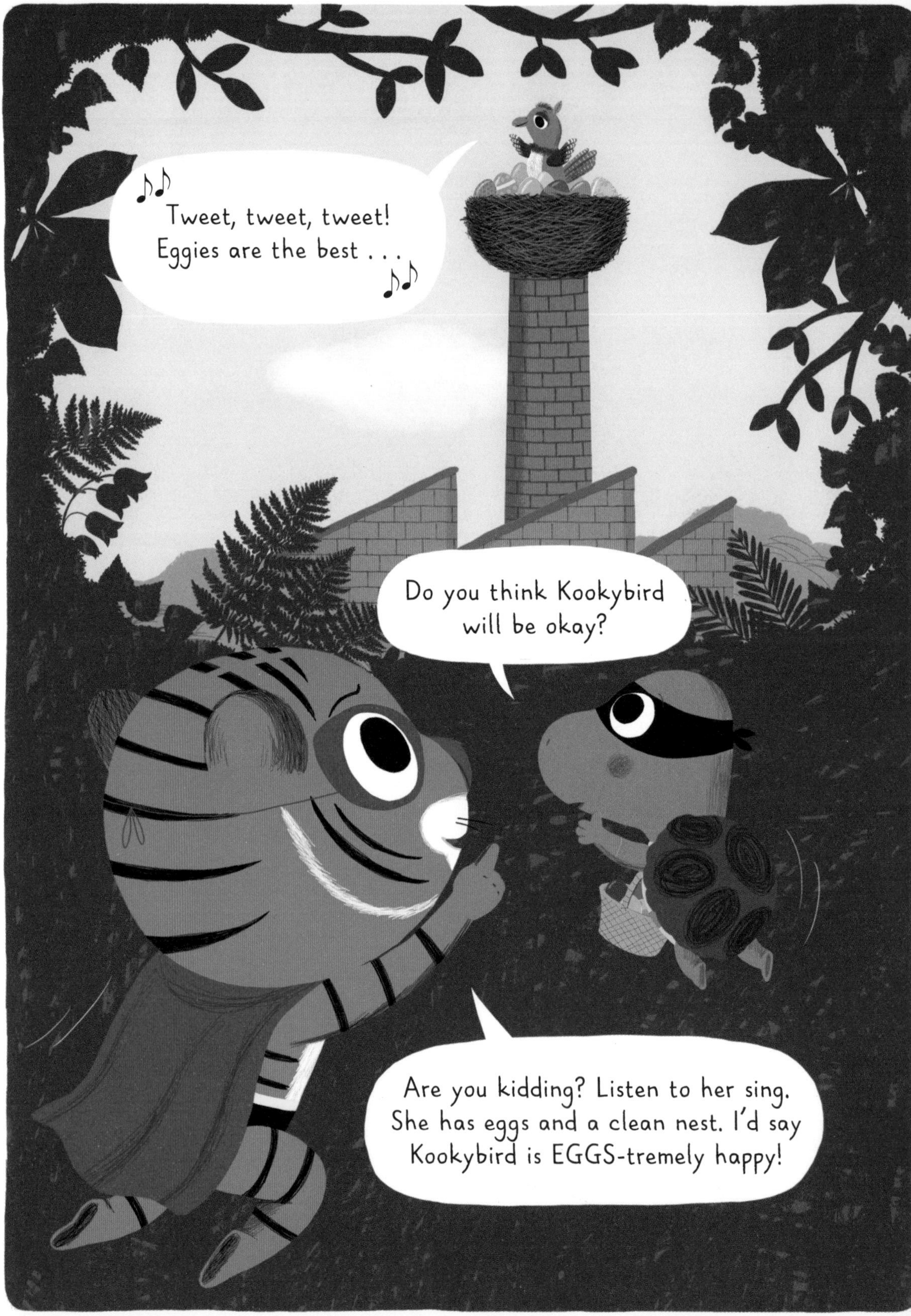
♪♪ Tweet, tweet, tweet! Eggies are the best . . . ♪♪
Do you think Kookybird will be okay?
Are you kidding? Listen to her sing. She has eggs and a clean nest. I'd say Kookybird is EGGS-tremely happy!

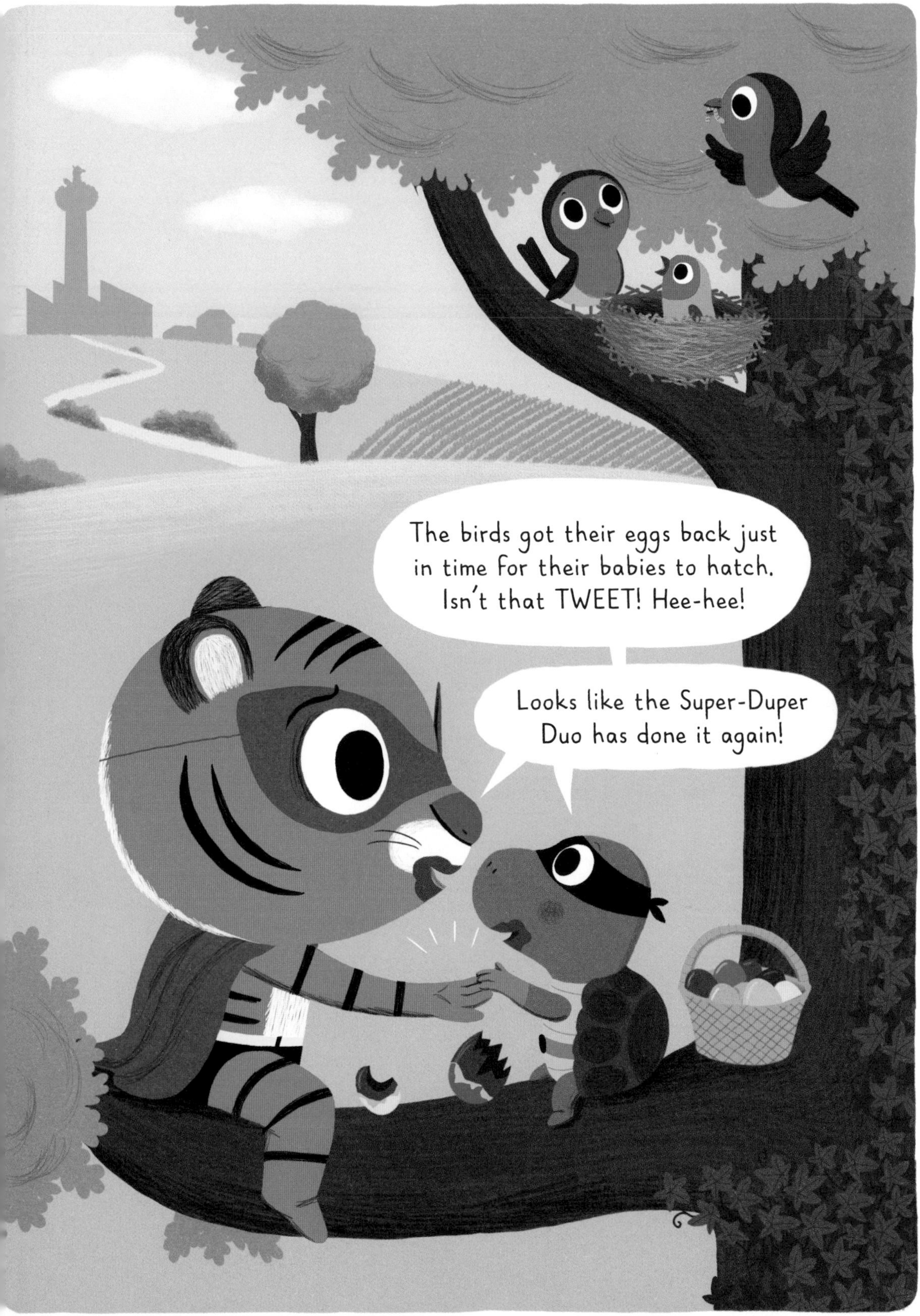
The birds got their eggs back just in time for their babies to hatch. Isn't that TWEET! Hee-hee!
Looks like the Super-Duper Duo has done it again!

SUPER-DUPER ANIMAL FACT

This Super-Duper Duo adventure features a made-up bird called a Kookybird. In the story, Kookybird takes other birds' eggs and keeps them in her nest. Guess what? There's a real-life bird called a cuckoo that does the opposite. Each spring, she lays as many as twenty eggs in other birds' nests. When the eggs hatch, the adoptive mothers raise the baby cuckoos as their own. Cuckoos are big birds and the chicks grow fast. In fact, after just three weeks, the young cuckoos are usually larger than their new moms. Now, that is truly kooky!